The stranger had an...aura about him,

and Sophie told herself she'd better get real.

This was the kind of man who could cause a hush simply by entering a room. The kind of man who made women wonder, who is he? What's he after? And is there any way I might have a chance with him?

Tall. Dark. Delectably menacing. Definitely not a man likely to be driven mad with desire by a woman who bought her dresses at yard sales and cut her own hair.

Sophie knew she ought to be suspicious of such obvious interest from a man like that.

And maybe she was suspicious. A little.

But, at the same time, her hopelessly romantic soul couldn't help but respond....

Dear Reader,

This September, four of our beloved authors pen irresistible sagas about lonesome cowboys, hard-luck heroines and love on the range! We've flashed these "Western-themed" romances with a special arch treatment. And additional treasures are provided to our readers by Christine Rimmer—a new JONES GANG book with an excerpt from her wonderful upcoming single title, *The Taming of Billy Jones,* as well as Marilyn Pappano's first Special Edition novel.

In *Every Cowgirl's Dream* by Arlene James, our THAT SPECIAL WOMAN! Kara Detmeyer is one feisty cowgirl who can handle just about anything—except the hard-edged cowboy who escorts her through a dangerous cattle drive. Don't miss this high-spirited adventure.

THE JONES GANG returns to Special Edition! In *A Hero for Sophie Jones,* veteran author Christine Rimmer weaves a poignant story about a ruthless hero who is transformed by love. And wedding bells are chiming in *The Mail-Order Mix-Up* by Pamela Toth, but can this jilted city sophisticate find true love? Speaking of mismatched lovers, a pregnant widow discovers forbidden passion with her late husband's half brother in *The Cowboy Take a Wife* by Lois Faye Dyer.

Rounding out the month, *Stranded on the Ranch* by Pat Warren features a sheltered debutante who finds herself snowbound with an oh-so-sexy rancher. And Marilyn Pappano brings us a bittersweet reunion romance between a reformed temptress and the wary lover she left behind in *Older, Wiser...Pregnant.* I hope you enjoy each and every story to come!

Sincerely,

Karen Taylor Richman
Senior Editor

Please address questions and book requests to:
Silhouette Reader Service
U.S.: 3010 Walden Ave., P.O. Box 1325, Buffalo, NY 14269
Canadian: P.O. Box 609, Fort Erie, Ont. L2A 5X3

CHRISTINE RIMMER

A HERO FOR SOPHIE JONES

Silhouette®

SPECIAL EDITION®

Published by Silhouette Books
America's Publisher of Contemporary Romance

What is it about those Joneses?
Every time I think I've written the last Jones Gang story,
another Jones pops up and says, "But what about me?"
This one's for all of you who have written me letters
asking for more.

SILHOUETTE BOOKS

ISBN 0-373-24196-8

A HERO FOR SOPHIE JONES

Copyright © 1998 by Christine Rimmer

CHRISTINE RIMMER

came to her profession the long way around. Before settling down to write about the magic of romance, she'd been an actress, a sales clerk, a janitor, a model, a phone sales representative, a teacher, a waitress, a playwright and an office manager. Now that she's finally found work that suits her perfectly, she insists she never had a problem keeping a job—she was merely gaining "life experience" for her future as a novelist. Those who know her best withhold comment when she makes such claims; they are grateful that she's at last found steady work. Christine is grateful, too—not only for the joy she finds in writing, but for what waits when the day's work is through: A man she loves who loves her right back and the privilege of watching their children grow and change day to day. She lives with her family in Oklahoma.

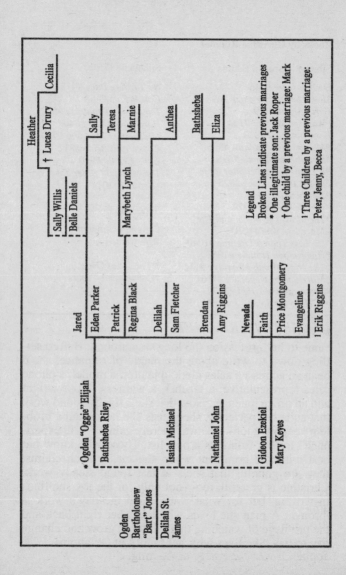

Legend

Broken Lines indicate previous marriages
* One illegitimate son: Jack Roper
† One child by a previous marriage: Mark
¹ One child by a previous marriage: Mark

¹ Three Children by a previous marriage:
  Peter, Jenny, Becca

Chapter One

The raven-haired stranger in the fifth row had eyes as black as his hair. Eyes that mesmerized. Eyes that managed to be both lazy looking and bold at the same time. Those eyes were locked right on her as Sophie B. Jones began introducing the evening's feature presentation.

"Welcome to the Mountain Star." Sophie smiled, a smile intended to include each and every one of the eighty-five people who sat in the ten rows of battered seats before her.

Though most of her guests smiled back, the dark-haired stranger did not. And he certainly seemed to be making himself at home, sitting there in an idle sprawl, an elbow braced on the seat arm and one long, graceful hand across his mouth. Thoughtfully, he brushed his index finger over his lips, an action that Sophie found extremely distracting.

Sophie made herself look past him. Smiling wider, she spread her arms in a gesture that embraced all of her guests at once. "I'm so glad you could make it, and I hope you enjoy this weekend's installment in what I like to think of as our Randi Wilding Film Retrospective."

From overhead, in the rafters of the old stone barn that housed Sophie's makeshift movie theater, came a soft cooing sound. Sophie glanced upward, then back out over the rows of expectant faces. "Pardon that pigeon." She lifted a shoulder in a what-can-I-tell-you shrug. "I thought I shooed him out of here this afternoon."

A low chuckle passed through the crowd. Sophie scanned the rows again, making eye contact, watching the little quirks of smiles come and go on the faces.

But not that one face.

Or, wait a minute—

Maybe he *had* smiled. She couldn't be sure, but it had seemed for a split second as if that sinfully sexy mouth of his had lifted at one corner.

And those bedroom eyes certainly did look interested—in a lot more than the evening's feature presentation at the Mountain Star. Those eyes seemed to speak to Sophie. They said they planned to get to know her. Intimately.

Up in the rafters, that pesky pigeon cooed once more.

And Sophie told herself that she'd better get real. The man had an...aura about him. He might be wearing chinos and a Polo shirt right now, but she just knew he had a closet full of Armani at home—wherever that was, some big city, she was sure.

It took no effort to picture him cruising around in

a limousine, behind windows tinted black. He was the kind of man who could cause a hush by simply entering a room. The kind of man who made women wonder: Who is he? What's he after? And is there any way I might have a chance with him?

Tall. Dark. Delectably menacing. Lord Byron and the vampire Lestat. Definitely not someone likely to be driven mad with desire by a woman who bought her dress at a yard sale and always cut her own hair.

Sophie ought to be suspicious of such obvious interest from a man like that, and she knew it.

And maybe she was suspicious. A little.

But at the same time, her hopelessly romantic soul couldn't help but respond, couldn't help feeling what those eyes said, *he* felt: attraction, plain and simple.

Sophie realized right then that the barn was way too silent. How long had she been standing there, pondering the possible agendas of Tall, Dark, Et Cetera, while her audience waited to hear about the show?

Something warm and fuzzy was making figure eights around her ankles. Grateful for an excuse to look away from all those staring eyes, she glanced down. "Eddie."

The gray tabby lifted his head. Yellow-green kitty eyes met hers. *"Rrreow?"*

She bent and scooped him up. He purred and nuzzled her neck. "You're a sweetheart, you are." Petting the cat, she dared to look out at the faces again— taking extreme care this time not to allow her gaze to linger on *him*.

"Let's see. Where was I? Oh, yes. Randi Wilding. As you all probably remember, she started out as just another gorgeous blonde—on the hit TV show, 'Eden

Beach.' She broke into movies a couple of years later. And now, at barely thirty years of age, she's become a megastar. Some still think of her as nothing more than a sex symbol, but those in the know are already calling her one of the great all-time actresses. She makes exciting, fast-paced movies that everyone wants to see, and she also makes each character she plays come alive on the screen.

"Tonight, you'll be seeing *Sagebrush and Desire.* It was Randi's second feature film. In it, she got to wear chaps and shoot a pair of pearl-handled Colts— not to mention deal with a passel of rustlers out to steal her herd. The word is that she did her own stunts, which I think you'll all agree is pretty amazing once you see the scene where she slides off the roof of a barn, turns a somersault in midair and lands square in the saddle on the back of her mustang mare—which bolts off at a dead run.

"Unfortunately—" Sophie smoothed Eddie's wiry fur "—that wasn't a big year for Westerns. *Sagebrush and Desire* remains Randi's only box-office flop. And you all know how I feel about box-office flops." Sophie paused, grinned, and scratched Eddie behind an ear. "I love them on principle. So tonight at the Mountain Star, I'm proud to present...Randi Wilding in *Sagebrush and Desire.*"

Friendly applause followed Sophie up the aisle. A shiver went through her as she passed the fifth row, but she didn't allow herself to turn and look into those dark eyes again.

Sin Riker watched the Jones woman as she strolled by with the gray cat in her arms. Her waterfall of honey brown hair shone gold in the glare from the fluorescent lights that hung from the rafters overhead. She looked sweet as a milkmaid in some sentimental old print.

He shifted a little, so he could watch her as she moved beyond him up the aisle. Beneath the hem of her worn flowered dress trailed about three inches of white cotton lace. On any other woman, it would have looked as if her slip was showing. But not on the Jones woman. On her, that border of lace looked just right.

At the top of the aisle, she let the cat down and climbed a ladder to what once must have been a hay-loft, but now clearly did duty as a projection booth. Sin watched that innocent white lace until it disappeared overhead, then he turned and faced the screen again.

She wasn't his type at all, of course. He preferred a more complex woman, one who could hold her own in the boardroom as well as the bedroom, one with a little darkness in her soul—to match his own.

In the rafters, the rogue pigeon fluttered his wings. The gray cat strolled down the center aisle, striped tail held high.

"I'm so glad we came," the elderly woman to Sin's right whispered to the gray-haired gent on her other side. The man took the woman's age-spotted hand. They shared a smile. "The Mountain Star is a special place," the woman said.

Sin had to agree. This impossible theater in a barn charmed him. He had no idea why. The awful, rickety seats must have been stolen from some condemned movie palace and the screen had a hole in the upper left-hand corner.

He should have found the place ridiculous. Yet he didn't. Not at all. It captivated him.

As did the Jones woman herself, with those big eyes and that sunny smile, all that bronze hair—and white lace showing beneath the hem of her skirt.

Not that this sudden, absurd fascination mattered one bit. Sin had no intention of allowing himself to be distracted by a pair of wide brown eyes. He had other, much more crucial business to transact with Sophie B. Jones.

The fluorescents overhead dimmed. Sin heard the rolling click of a projector starting up. He shifted in his seat again, trying to get reasonably comfortable, as the show began.

When intermission came, Sophie set her ancient projector to rewind the first reel. Then she climbed down the ladder to handle the concession stand.

Though Sophie had two full-time employees and a part-time maid to help her at the Mountain Star Resort, she ran the theater herself. Her guests—both the ones who took rooms in the main house and the folks who drove in from town just to see the show—loved it that way. They bought their tickets from her, she served them their refreshments, and before they saw the show, they got to hear her opinion of it.

That night the dark stranger bought a bowl of popcorn. Myra Bailey, the Mountain Star's cook, popped the corn up fresh before the show. Sophie served it in plastic bowls.

The stranger also bought a bottle of spring water.

"That's three, four, five—and five makes ten." Sophie counted change into that elegant hand. She made the mistake of glancing up, of meeting those deep dark eyes. Instantly all rational thought sailed right out of her mind. She could only stare. They just didn't make men like this anymore—if they ever really had.

He tucked the change into a pocket, his mouth barely lifting at the corner the way it had earlier, in the slightest insinuation of a smile. "I suppose you're going to want this bowl back."

She watched his lips move, and wondered vaguely what he was talking about. He prompted in a teasing whisper, "The bowl—do you want it back?"

She had to cough to make her throat open enough for words to come out. "Oh, yes. The bowl. Yes, I would. Like it back. It's recyclable. I wash them and use them all over again."

He waited, not smiling, just looking, a look that made her feel warm and weak and positively wonderful. She had no idea what he was waiting for, but it didn't seem to matter much.

Then he asked, "Where should I put it?"

She gestured way too wildly, almost whacking him one on his sculpted jaw. "Over there. On that little table by the double doors…"

He nodded. "Good enough." And then he smiled. Really smiled.

It was nine-fifteen at night and outside an August moon was shining down, but to Sophie the sun came up at that moment. Even when he turned, carrying his popcorn and water, and headed for the curtains that separated her concession area from the rest of the barn, she still felt as if she'd been blinded by the bright light of a new day.

It was ludicrous. And she knew it. Hopeless romantic or not, she had to get a grip here.

"How about a pear nectar?" the next fellow in line asked.

Sophie gave him a brisk, very professional smile. "Pear nectar it is."

Through the final reel, as Randi Wilding relentlessly hunted down and disposed of all the rustlers who'd dared to do their dirty work on her ranch, Sophie B. Jones gave herself a good talking-to.

Life, after all, was not a movie. In real life, handing a man his change should not be a transcendent experience. And it *hadn't* been a transcendent experience—except in her own suddenly hyperactive imagination, which she was squelching as of now.

By the time the final credits rolled, Sophie felt she had herself under reasonable control. She climbed down the ladder from the booth-hayloft, pulled back the curtains that masked her concession stand and opened the big barn doors wide.

Then, by the light of that almost full August moon, with another of her cats in her arms, she stood in the open doors and said goodbye to all of her guests personally, just as she always did.

Among those guests was Oggie Jones. At least once a month, he drove down from the tiny nearby town of North Magdalene for an evening at the movies.

"Quite a shoot-'em-up tonight, gal," Oggie declared when his turn came to say goodbye.

Sophie let the cat slide to the ground and held out her arms. The old sweetheart allowed her to hug him. He smelled of those awful cigars he was always smoking, but Sophie didn't really mind. She simply adored him. The first time he'd come to the Mountain

Star, he'd told her to call him Uncle Oggie. And she had from then on, because it seemed so natural. Three years ago, he'd invited her to North Magdalene, a half hour's drive from the Mountain Star, northeast on old Highway Forty-Nine. She'd met his whole family, his four sons and his daughter, their spouses and their children. They'd welcomed her as if she were one of them. Since then, she'd returned to visit often.

She wasn't sure what it was about Oggie, but whenever she saw him, she always experienced the loveliest rising of affection in her heart—as if he really *were* her uncle, instead of just a sweet old character who shared her last name and her fondness for offbeat movies.

"Oh, Uncle Oggie, I hope you enjoyed yourself."

"I always enjoy myself. It's the only way to live." He leaned in closer, lowered his raspy voice and wiggled his grizzled eyebrows in the direction of Tall, Dark and Dangerous—who just happened to be standing near the concession counter showing no inclination to leave. "Someone's watching you."

Sophie shrugged—casually she hoped. "I haven't a clue why."

Oggie's small wise eyes seemed to bore holes right through her. Then he grinned. "Somethin' tells me that you ain't gonna be clueless for long."

And Oggie was right. After all the other guests had gone, Sophie's brooding stranger remained—which, Sophie told herself, didn't matter one bit.

She had work to do. Turning to the small table in the corner, she scooped up two stacks of used popcorn bowls. Then she started toward the man at the counter, who just kept on leaning there, watching her approach.

When she got about a foot from him, she paused. "Show's over." She tried to sound breezy and unconcerned.

"I know." He didn't move. He looked completely relaxed, as if he hung around after the show all the time—waiting for her.

"Everyone's gone," she said, trying again. "Except you."

"I noticed."

She decided she was going to have to be more direct. "Now *you* have to go—and I have to clean up."

He only went on looking at her, an assessing kind of look, a look that made her skin feel warm and her heart beat way too fast.

She told her heart to settle down—and held out the used popcorn bowls. "Well, fine. If you're going to hang around, you might as well make yourself useful."

He gave her another of those almost smiles of his. Then he shrugged and accepted the bowls.

She pointed at the curtain behind the counter. "Take those right through there."

Her stranger was standing by the double metal sink, still holding his share of the bowls, when she joined him in the small alcove behind the curtain.

"Just drop them in the sink."

He did as she instructed, then stood out of the way as she piled the rest of the bowls on top, squirted in a stream of dish soap and started the water running. With a swiftness born of long practice, she began washing bowls and dropping them into the empty half of the sink.

Her stranger caught on fast. He flipped the faucet

to the right, turned on the water and reached for a soapy bowl. When he had it rinsed, he held it up and quirked an eyebrow.

"Just set them right there. They'll dry by themselves."

He put the bowl on the grooved steel drainboard and picked up the next one, and then the next. From the corner of her eye, she could see those beautiful hands, working as efficiently as her own. *The Prince of Darkness does the dishes,* she thought, and had to stifle a burst of foolish laughter. His watch winked at her, platinum and gold, a watch that must have cost more than the Dodge Caravan she was still making payments on.

A few minutes later, Sophie dried her hands and then passed him the towel.

"What else?" He hung the towel back on its peg.

"Sweeping the aisles and taking out the trash."

"Hand me the broom."

She leaned back against the sink and slid him a sideways glance. "You really would, wouldn't you?"

"Sweep the floor? Why not?" He waited. When she didn't move, he added, "But I'll need a broom to do it."

She shuffled her feet and crossed her arms. "Well, I guess I just can't."

"Can't what?"

"Ask a total stranger to do my scut work."

He looked amused. "You didn't ask, I volunteered."

"No. I handed you those bowls. I told you to make yourself useful."

He laughed. It was a deep, very masculine sound.

It sent lovely warm shivers racing right beneath the surface of her skin.

She said, "Look. Never mind. I can do it in the morning."

He shrugged, leaned on the other side of the sink and crossed his arms over his chest in a mirror of her own pose.

She looked down at her sandaled feet. When she dared to glance his way again, those dark eyes were waiting for her.

She had to know. "All right. Who *are* you?"

He answered without hesitation. "My name is Sinclair. Sinclair Riker."

It took Sophie a minute to believe what she'd heard. Then she barely managed to stifle a gasp.

The man beside her chuckled. "From the look on your face, I'd say the locals have been filling your ears with old gossip."

Sophie struggled to compose herself. "I...of course, I've heard of you—that is, if you're the same Sinclair Riker whose family once owned this ranch."

"That's me."

Sophie looked down at her sandals again. The old story was such a sad one. And from the way she'd heard it, he had been a vulnerable child of six when the grim events took place.

Not sure if he'd welcome a direct mention of the tragedy, Sophie ventured, "I think I heard that your mother took you away from here—to Southern California, wasn't it?"

"That's right, but my mother's been dead for a few years now."

Sophie murmured an expression of sympathy.

He shrugged. "It was all a long time ago."

What did he mean by that? A long time since his mother had died? A long time since his father had lost the ranch—and then hung himself in despair? His eyes told her nothing, though she wanted to know everything.

He turned away and stared off toward the curtain that led back to the main part of the barn.

Sophie reminded herself—again—that they'd only just met. She had no right at all to expect him to tell her things he probably didn't even like thinking about.

She asked carefully, "Are you...all right?"

He faced her again. His eyes had a strange, hot light in them.

Sophie thought she understood what he felt. "You've wondered about your family home, haven't you? You wanted to come and see for yourself what happened to it."

He didn't answer, only went on staring at her with those burning dark eyes.

She began to feel uncomfortable. "What is it? Have I got it all wrong?"

He shook his head. "No, not at all. The truth is, you've figured me out."

It was a lie.

Sin Riker knew exactly what had happened to his family home.

He owned it. The sale had been finalized two weeks before.

And now, he intended to claim what was his, to buy out this innocent and eliminate the peculiar enterprise she called the Mountain Star.

Chapter Two

Sin stared into those gorgeous brown eyes—eyes utterly lacking in guile. Eyes that said she simply wanted to know about him.

What the hell was it about her?

She wasn't his type at all.

He found himself thinking of Willa, with her black hair like a swatch of silk and her brittle, knowing laugh. Willa Tweed was his kind of woman: clever, ambitious—and sexy as hell. A talented interior designer, Willa had handled the decorating of several office buildings for him. She'd kept his interest for over a year, both in and out of bed. She'd seemed the perfect match for him, so he had asked her to marry him.

And yet, when she'd called the whole thing off, he hadn't found it difficult at all to let her go. Which, he supposed, was just more proof of his total lack of character.

As if he needed more proof.

The Jones woman's generous mouth bloomed in an artless smile. "I understand completely," she assured him. "I love this place. If I ever had to leave it, I know I'd be drawn back again—just to see it, to know that it's still here."

Watching her smile, listening to her sympathize when no sympathy was called for, Sin knew he should call a halt right then. She betrayed herself so easily. Those eyes of hers didn't know how to lie. And she was warming to him, starting to *like* him. She had a sunny, trusting nature. In no time at all, she would be telling him all about herself—all the facts of her life that he already knew.

There was no point at all in indulging in this flirtation with her.

Except that he couldn't seem to stop himself.

"Hello, are you in there?" Sophie teased. To her, it seemed as if Sinclair had been standing there, regarding her intently, saying nothing, for about half a century.

He gave her a rueful smile. "I'm here, all right."

"Good."

They shared a warm glance, standing there side by side against the steel sink. Sophie recalled how she'd lectured herself about him, up in the hayloft during the second reel.

But now that all seemed so silly. She wanted to get to know him, and she could think of no reason why she shouldn't.

Especially now that she knew his name.

Sinclair Riker. She still couldn't quite believe it.

Since the first time she'd heard the sad story of the Rikers, Sophie had wondered about them, *felt* for them really, to have owned this beautiful piece of land and then to have lost it. For the boy, Sinclair, her sympathy had gone even deeper. He'd been so young to lose so much. Her heart went out to him.

"Your name is Sophie—isn't it?" His tone chided, but very gently.

And Sophie felt a little ashamed. Here she'd been so suspicious of him, and yet she was the one who hadn't even provided her name. "Yes. Sophie. Sophie B. Jones. Most folks just call me Sophie B."

"*B* for?"

"Bernadette."

He made a low noise in his throat. "Don't tell me. It was your grandmother's name, right?"

She shook her head. "Why would you think that?"

"Because it was *my* grandmother's name."

"You're kidding."

"No." His gaze swept over her from head to toe. "So if it wasn't your grandmother's name, then whose?"

"My mother chose it. From an old movie. *The Song of Bernadette,* starring Jennifer Jones. Ever heard of it?"

He shook his head.

"Bernadette was a nun, I believe. In the movie."

"A nun," he murmured. "I should have known."

For that, she made a face at him. "I remind you of a nun?"

"Did I say that?"

"You didn't have to."

He leaned her way then, and lowered his voice. "I have to admit, I asked around a little."

She wasn't surprised. "About the ranch?"

He nodded. "Everyone I talked to seemed to know all about Ms. Sophie B. Jones and the Mountain Star Resort."

She wrinkled up her nose. "I hope they only said nice things."

"Only terrific things." He reached out and took her hand. His touch sent tiny, lovely tingles all through her. With great care, he wrapped her fingers in the crook of his arm. It felt absolutely wonderful to have him do that—as well as absolutely right. "Come on. Show me what you've done with my father's ranch."

Beyond the barn doors, the August moon shone down through the pines. A gentle breeze stirred the branches, creating haunting plays of shadow and silvery light. Somewhere off by the small creek that wound over the property, they could hear the night songs of crickets and frogs.

"It *is* a beautiful place," Sinclair said.

In lieu of a reply, Sophie squeezed his arm, then suggested, "How about the stables first?"

Before he could answer, two figures materialized out of the shadows not far from the barn doors.

"Sophie B.," a male voice said.

Sophie felt Sinclair's lean arm stiffen under her hand. She gave that arm another squeeze. "It's all right. These are friends."

The two came into the light: a man and a woman— well, a boy and a girl, really. Neither could have been much out of their teens. Sophie felt pretty sure of their names. "Hello, Ben. And Melody." Each carried a bedroll and a backpack. Even in the kind light of the moon, their jeans and T-shirts looked worn.

Melody laughed. "We scared you, huh?"

"Never," Sophie replied.

"We meant to get here for the show, but we were too late."

More likely, they didn't have the money for the tickets. Sophie would have let them in anyway, but they were proud kids, kids who didn't like taking charity—especially not for non-necessities like movies.

Sophie shrugged. "Maybe next time."

"Yeah. Next time. Cool."

Sophie knew what they wanted. "Campground's open, as far as I'm concerned."

Ben looked relieved. "Thanks. We're really beat. Come on, Mel."

They hoisted their packs and started off in the opposite direction from the main house. Sophie called after them. "Stop in and say hi to Myra tomorrow, why don't you?"

Melody called back, "Thanks, Sophie B. You're the best."

Sinclair spoke. "The 'campground' is open?" His tone seemed to mock her.

Sophie turned to look at him. But the moon was behind him. His face lay in shadow. She couldn't see his expression. "I call it a campground," she said, "but it's really just a nice, grassy spot with trees all around. On a mild night like this one, it's a great place to spread a sleeping bag." She pointed. "It's just over that rise there."

"Those two have nowhere else to go, is that it?" There was a definite chill in his voice, she was sure of that now.

She answered gently. "I don't know if they have

anywhere else to go. All I know is that they need a place to stay for tonight and I can provide that easily.''

"If you let people move in on you, you're just asking for trouble.''

She didn't believe that and she never would. "They'll be on their way in the morning."

"How can you be sure?''

"It always works out that way. The street people who come here know how to behave.''

"You've been lucky.''

"I suppose I have,'' she admitted. "But it's not only that.''

"Oh, no? What else, then?''

She shot him a grin. "I have to tell you, I never let skeptics like you get to me.''

"All right, then." His voice had changed again, lost its cold edge. "Why won't you share your secret—if it's more than plain luck?''

"Because you'll only laugh if I tell you.''

"No.'' He put his hand over hers. "I won't laugh. I swear.''

His touch sent those shivers zinging through her all over again. She couldn't help relenting. "All right. In my experience, people tend to fulfill my expectations of them. So I always make it a point to keep my expectations good and high.''

He said nothing for a moment. Then he let out a breath. "As I said, you've been lucky.''

"Call it luck if you want to. But it works for me.'' She tugged on his arm. "Now, come on. The stables are waiting.''

They went down a slate path, beneath the leafy shelter of a double row of maples, until they came to a rambling woodsided building from which a series of linked corrals branched off. Inside the stables, Sophie turned on the lights and they walked between the rows of stalls.

Sophie said, "I know your father used to raise horses here. Morgans, mostly, weren't they?"

"Yes. We lost them all, though. They took them away when they kicked us out of the house."

Another wave of sympathy washed through her. How could he have borne all those losses at such a young age? "It must have been awful for you."

He studied her face for a moment. "As I said..."

"I know. It was a long time ago."

Sophie paused to stroke the forehead of a friendly roan gelding and explained that none of the horses belonged to the Mountain Star. "We run a boarding service for people who don't have the space to keep their own horses. Some of the owners allow guests at the main house to ride their animals, under certain conditions—and for a fee, of course."

"Certain conditions?"

"Caleb Taggart, who runs the stables for me, has to check them out first, see if they know how to ride and how to treat a horse."

Right then, Caleb, who was six feet five and broad as an oak, appeared from the apartment he'd fixed up for himself off the tack room. He loomed huge and imposing before them. "Everything okay, Sophie B.?" He looked at her guest with stolid wariness.

"Everything is fine." She performed the introductions and the two men shook hands.

"Caleb helps me keep the grounds in order, as well as running the stables," she explained a few minutes later, when they were on their way to the main house. "He's a genius with horses."

"A *large* genius," Sin added. "And he seems very protective of you."

"He is." She grinned. "Both large *and* protective. He's worked for me from the beginning, which was five years ago."

They stopped at the edge of the wide, sloping lawn in front of the main house. Sophie told him more about the Mountain Star. "I have a fifteen-year lease on five acres—the crucial five acres we're standing on, which includes the main house, the barn, the stables and corrals, and the guest house, too, where I live. The local teachers' association owns it all—or at least they did."

His shadowy gaze was on her. "They *did?* Past tense?"

Something in his tone bothered her, though she couldn't have said what, and a small tremor of alarm skittered through her—a sudden sense that all was not as it should be.

But then she told herself not to overreact. She felt apprehensive about this particular subject, that was all. It had nothing to do with Sinclair.

She'd received the notice from the San Francisco bank just a week before, and since then she'd been trying not to stew over what it might mean to the Mountain Star. She'd asked around, but the sale had been accomplished through intermediaries, and no one seemed to know much about the new owner.

She explained, "Some corporation owns the ranch now. In San Francisco, I think. I got a letter about it just last week. It said to send the lease payments to a Bay Area bank, and make the checks out to something called Inkerris, Incorporated.''

''*Inkerris,* Incorporated?''

''Yes. Have you heard of it?''

He shrugged, which she took to mean ''no.''

She sighed. ''I have to admit, I wasn't surprised to hear about a new owner.''

''Why not?''

''The teachers' association has been wanting to sell for a long time. They bought the ranch because they had a plan to build tract homes here. But somehow the plan never got off the ground. That's when I came in. They wanted some kind of return on their investment. I made them an offer.''

Two serpentine boulders flanked the base of the walk that led up to the main house. Sophie perched on one, smoothed her skirt and wrapped her hands around her knees. ''It's worked out great for me. I have the run of the rest of the place—all nine hundred and ninety-five acres. A lot of the guests like to hike. And the folks who board their horses with us appreciate the convenience of being able to just come in, saddle up and ride for miles without seeing any houses or highways.''

Sinclair stood over her, his hands in his pockets. ''It does sound like a good deal for you.''

''It has been. Too bad the teachers' association didn't feel the same way.''

''You couldn't expect them to hold onto a losing investment forever.''

''Of course not.'' She looked up at him, and they shared a smile. ''I only *wished* that they would.''

In a sleek, easy motion, he dropped to a crouch

before her, so he was the one looking up. "You love it here, don't you?"

She nodded, thinking again how unbelievably good-looking he was, a dark angel, so lean and fine. "I've been fortunate," she said, "to have all this, though I know it isn't really mine. I would have bought it myself—if I could have afforded it. But I'm never likely to get that kind of money together." She smoothed her skirt again. "Oh, well. Maybe in ten years, when my lease is up, whatever corporation owns it then will let me renew."

Thinking about the tenuous nature of her hold on the Mountain Star always bothered Sophie. And lately, since the letter from the San Francisco bank, it disturbed her more than ever.

She looked off, beyond Sinclair's shoulder. In the center of the lawn, she could see the fountain. Caleb had put in a good deal of work on that fountain, cleaning out rusted pipes so it would work again. At its center stood a statue of a little girl, holding out her skirt to capture the shimmering streams of water as they cascaded down. The little girl was laughing— even by moonlight, her delight came across. Sophie loved that statue, and the sight of it cheered her.

Pointless to worry, needless to fret, her aunt Sophie always used to say....

"Hey." The man before her reached out. His fingers whispered along the line of her cheek. She forgot her worries—she even forgot the laughing little girl— as she met his eyes again.

Incredible, she thought, how good it felt, to have him touch her. As if it were the most natural thing in the world.

So strange. She felt so close to him. As if they'd

known each other forever, as if they had a history of shared experience, as if she'd long ago grown accustomed to his touch.

Accustomed, but never weary of it.

Oh, no. She could never grow weary of his touch. Featherlight, it was. And at the same time, like a brand. Burning...

Gentle as a breath, he touched her hair. Right then, his eyes seemed full of timeless mystery as the Sierra night around them. "Do you really think that's likely?"

What were they talking about? She couldn't for the life of her remember. "Do I think what's likely?"

"That you'll convince some faceless corporation to renew your lease when your time here runs out?"

She knew it wasn't. Only a combination of good fortune and good timing had made the Mountain Star a reality. She shook her head. "But I have what I want now. And as for the future—a girl can dream, can't she?"

"Absolutely." Once more, his fingers touched her cheek. And then they fell away. He rose above her again, with the same seamless ease of movement as before. She felt regret, as if some precious impossible intimacy had been lost.

And then she stood as well, smoothing the back of her skirt as she did. "Shall we go in?"

He frowned.

She knew immediately what that frown meant: he didn't want to go in.

And no wonder. There were probably hard memories for him in that house. The old story went that the boy, Sinclair, had been the one who found his father's body—in one of the two attic rooms, dangling from a rafter beam.

"Would you rather just skip the house?" she suggested gingerly.

"Of course not." His voice had turned cold as a night in midwinter. "Let's go." He held out his arm for her again. After a moment's hesitation, she took it. They started up the walk, past the bubbling fountain with its laughing little girl, toward the house where the man beside her had spent the first six years of his life.

Riker cottage, as the house had always been called, was a steep-roofed structure built of natural stone, with redbrick trim in the dormers and around the window casements. Sinclair said nothing as they went under the brick-lined arch that framed the front door.

Sophie had learned already that he was a man prone to silences. But his silence now had a strange edge to it, an edge she didn't like at all. She almost suggested for the second time that they not go in. But she knew from his response a moment ago that it would do no good.

There was nothing else for it. She reached for the iron latch on the heavy oak door.

The door opened on a large central foyer. From there, a switch-back staircase led up to the guest rooms. Twin parlors branched off to either side.

Sophie showed Sinclair the ground floor first. In the east parlor, they found two guests playing chess. Sinclair nodded when she introduced him to the chess players—a brief, aloof nod. Her guests seemed to take no offense to his coldness. They bent over their game again right away. But it did bother Sophie—because she sensed his chilly manner was only a cover-up for distress.

He did not want to be here, she knew it. She could feel it in her bones. He said nothing when she showed him the library, where his father's books still stood in the tall, glass-fronted cases.

In an effort to fill the ominous silence that seemed to emanate from him, Sophie talked about the small changes she'd made. "I couldn't bear to tear out the wainscotting," she said of the shoulder-high paneling that lined the walls of most of the rooms. "But the old wallpaper had to go. Cabbage roses on a black background, if you remember. It was just way too dark. I chose only light colors for the ceilings and upper walls. I think it helps."

"Yes," he said flatly. "It helps."

In the kitchen, he seemed to relax a little—enough to point out deficiencies of which she was already fully aware. "How old is that stove?"

"Too old," she confessed. "Myra, the cook, is always saying rude things about it."

"Myra is right." He looked in the too-small refrigerator and ran a hand over the chipped counter tiles. "You could use a serious upgrade here."

"Tell me about it."

"So why haven't you done something?"

She had. She'd gotten some estimates. Even without the chef-style range and refrigerator Myra wanted, a remodel of the kitchen would cost at least fifteen thousand dollars. It was fifteen thousand more than she had.

But that wasn't his problem, so she only said, "I'll get around to it. Eventually."

He looked at her then, one of those looks she couldn't read at all. "You're sure about that?"

"I like to think positive."

"I noticed." It sounded like a criticism, but she let it pass.

She led him up the narrow, dark back stairs next. "I can't show you much of the other two floors," she explained as they climbed. "This is my peak season and all of the rooms are occupied. But we can at least take a quick look around."

He followed behind her, saying nothing. She didn't like his silence. It spoke to her of a deep unease. He did not want to be here, and yet he was forcing himself to stay, to carry on with this unnecessary tour.

Finally she couldn't stand it. She stopped midway and turned to him in the confined space.

"Are you sure you wouldn't rather forget about this?"

He just looked at her, his face a blank.

"Sinclair? Can you hear me?"

Sin did hear. And he wanted to reply. He wanted to tell her that he was fine, to order her to get going, get it over with, show him the rest of the damn place and be done with it.

But somehow, he couldn't make any words come out. Too many memories swirled around him: smells and sights and sounds. Fleeting impressions of the life he'd once lived here.

The smell of his mother's cinnamon cookies baking. Even in their last days here, when money got so tight they rarely had meat, she still baked those cookies. For him. Because he loved them.

Cinnamon cookies. And roses.

His mother had loved roses. She would pick them

from the poorly tended garden, where they grew in a wild tangle, and put them in vases all over the house.

And stories.

His father used to tell him stories. About great-grandfather Riker, who had labored in the gold mines, deep in the earth, alongside the Cornishmen who came all the way from England to work the mother lode. Great-Grandfather Riker had died in a cave-in, but not before he'd borne a son, Sinclair—for whom Sin had later been named. The first Sinclair Riker had grown up smart and lucky and used every penny he could scrape together to buy land, to create the Riker Ranch.

Which Anthony had lost in barely a decade after the first Sinclair's death.

Yes, his father's voice. He could hear it now. Telling the old stories.

And his father's laughter, deep and rich, he could hear that, as well.

And his mother, he could hear her, too, singing to him.

She used to sing all the time, when he was little. She would move through the dark rooms of the cottage, filling them with roses, making them seem light with her smiles and her songs. But then had come the bad day, the day they had to leave their home forever, the day when he stumbled down from the attic, unable to speak.

His mother had been standing at the window in the west parlor, staring out at the sunshine and the overgrown lawn. He had run to her, buried his face against her skirt.

Her soft arms went around him. She knelt down. "Sinclair. Darling. What's happened? You look as if you've seen a ghost.'' He backed from her embrace, grabbed for her pretty white hand. Ridiculous squawking noises were coming from his mouth.

''Sweetheart, slow down. What is it? What's wrong?''

He gave up on trying to talk and started yanking on her hand.

''All right, I'm coming. I'm coming. Settle down.''

He ran then, through the hall to the kitchen, up the back stairs—these very stairs he stood on now—pulling his mother along behind, all the way, up and up, to what used to be the maid's room, long ago when they could afford a maid.

When she saw it, she screamed. A terrible, never-ending scream of despair.

And after that day, she never sang again.

A cool hand touched his face. ''Sinclair?''

He realized he was clammy under the arms and across his chest. He lifted a hand to swipe at his brow. It came away dripping with his own sweat.

''Let's go outside,'' the Jones woman said. She stood so close to him. God, the scent of her. Like sunshine and flowers, like something so clean and fresh. The reality of her, the *life* in her, seemed to reach out to him....

He put out both hands and took her around the waist. She gasped. He felt her stiffen under his touch, but he couldn't help himself. He yanked her tight against him and buried his face in the thick, sweet tangle of her hair.

Chapter Three

Sophie's first instinct was to push him away.

Her second was to gather him close.

She never acted on the first. It passed as swiftly as her own sharply indrawn gasp of dismay. She was already wrapping her arms around him as they fell together against the wall of the stairwell. His lean body shook under her hands.

"It's okay," she murmured, so low the words were barely audible, even to herself. "Shh. It's all right."

He held on, tight enough to squeeze the breath from her lungs. His heart beat fast and furious, in time with her own. His face pressed first against her hair, then lower, into the curve of her neck. She felt his mouth on her skin in a caress that wasn't so much a kiss as a hungry demand for shelter from the chaos inside his own mind and heart.

He needed to touch someone. He needed someone to hold him.

She understood that. She let him touch. And she held him tight, his body branding all along hers, hot and needful, pleading without words.

How long they stood like that, pressed against the wall, she couldn't have said. Gradually, though, his heartbeat calmed and his breathing slowed. His hard grip loosened. She found she could breathe again.

He lifted a hand and stroked her hair. She felt his lips move at her neck in a tender kiss, sweet with gratitude.

And then at last he pulled away, grasping her shoulders and stepping back in the cramped space. His baffled gaze found hers. "God. I'm sorry." A dark curse escaped him. "I don't know what—"

She reached across the distance he'd made, put a finger on his mouth. It felt so soft. Tender. Bruised. "Let's just go. Outside."

He stared at her for an endless moment—and then he captured her hand. "Yes. Now."

He turned and headed down the stairs, into the kitchen, through the pantry, and out the door there—fleeing that house, and pulling her after him.

They ran across the rear lawn and into the grove of oaks that grew just beyond the edge of the grass. There, at last, he stopped. He threw himself back against one thick twisted trunk. He still held her hand. He gave a tug.

She fell against him. And she dared to laugh, a nervous sound, breathless and vivid at the same time. "Sinclair?"

He took her face in his hands and tipped it up so

the dappling of moonlight through the branches showed her to him.

He felt so angry suddenly. Angry, exposed—and aroused, as well.

He pressed himself against her, wanting her to feel his desire—half hoping she would jerk away in outrage, close herself off from him—and thus allow him to close himself off from her.

But she didn't jerk away. Her body seemed to melt into his.

"I don't know you," he said, each word careful, determined.

Her soft, full mouth invited him. She said his name again—his grandfather's name, the name she knew him by. "Sinclair..."

"I don't know you." He said it through clenched teeth that time.

She smiled, the softest, most beautiful smile. "You know me."

"No..."

"Yes."

He lowered his mouth to hers, to stop her from saying that—and discovered his error immediately. Her mouth was as soft as it looked. And as incredibly sweet. He moaned, the sound echoing inside his own head, as he plunged his tongue into that sweetness.

He was out of control, gone. Finished. Not himself. Not himself at all.

He took her by the arms, hard—and pushed her away. She let out one soft, bewildered cry—and then she just looked at him through those eyes that reproached him at the same time as they seemed to say that they understood.

She flinched. He realized he was holding her arms

too tightly, hurting her. He let go. She stumbled a little, righted herself, and then gave him more distance, stepping backward until she could lean against another tree, not far from him.

For a time, all he knew were her eyes through the night—watching. Waiting. And the night sounds—crickets and plaintive birdsongs, some small creature moving about, rustling in the dried late-summer grass nearby.

Slowly he came back to himself. More or less. "I'm sorry," he told her again, knowing as the pitiful words passed his lips that they weren't nearly enough. "I don't know what happened in there. Or just now, either."

She waved away his apologies. "It doesn't matter."

"Damn it, it does matter." The words came out low, but hard with leashed fury.

She only leaned against that tree, looking at him. He wanted to cover the short distance between them, grab her again, and shake her until she admitted what a bastard he was. But somehow he contained himself.

She just went on staring, those wide eyes so sweet, full of understanding and patience.

"Don't," he commanded.

She winced at his harshness. "Don't what?"

"Don't look at me like that."

And she immediately turned her head and looked away.

There was silence, but for the sounds of the night.

After a few moments, she turned her face to him again. "Would you like to see my favorite spot?"

Impossible though it was, he knew immediately the spot she meant: a certain place along the nearby creek. Past the oak grove, around the bend—a tiny grotto, green and magical, with willows growing all around and yellow-green moss like a blanket on the ground. He had found the place himself as a child. And loved it. And thought of it as his.

Anger arrowed through him again. Who the hell was she to choose his spot as hers?

"Sinclair." Her knowing eyes seemed to see right through him. "It's all right. All of it. Really."

He shook his head and looked away from her, because it wasn't all right. It was crazy. This whole thing—the wide-eyed woman and the August night, what had happened in that damn house and what was happening inside him now. Never in a million years would he have imagined that tonight would go like this.

No. Tonight was supposed to have been nothing more than a scouting expedition, a chance to check out his adversary in person before she even knew that he planned to reclaim what was his at any cost.

Sin slumped against the oak tree. Short seconds ago, he had been furious. Now his fury had fizzled to nothing. In its place remained a raw awareness of his own idiocy.

He'd grabbed the woman, in the house and here—and forced himself on her, completely out of nowhere. And what point could there possibly be in becoming irate because she favored the same section of creek he had liked as a child? It was ridiculous.

Ten to one, he'd learn it wasn't the same spot he remembered anyway. After all, decades had passed. The creekbed would have shifted in high-water years. The place he remembered wouldn't even exist anymore.

"Please." She came away from her tree trunk and took two hesitant steps toward him. "Come with me." She extended her hand.

He took it. He *was* an idiot. No doubt about it. A shiver went through him—from the sudden breeze that had come up, he told himself, a breeze that chilled him as it dried the sweat of his preposterous anguish from his skin.

"This way." She was already turning toward the creek.

He stumbled along behind her, dazed—spellbound in spite of himself. Out of the oak grove and into an open field of tall, dry grass that made her calf-length skirt whisper sweetly as she ran. He looked up. A million stars winked back at him, jewels of light strewn across a midnight ground of sky.

As a child, he had run like this. Under this same Sierra sky in high summer, with the moon benign and shining white, smiling down on him.

The field sloped away and they came to the creek. It sparkled in the moonlight, its dark surface glistening as it fled over the rocky bed beneath.

She turned to him, granted him one brief, conspiratorial glance. "Not far now." And then she was off again, along the bank, pulling him after.

Within moments, they came to the spot. And it was the same. Exactly the same as he remembered it.

She pulled him up onto the big black rock at the very edge of the stream, the rock he used to sit on for hours as little boy. "Here," she said. "Right here. Sit down." He obeyed her command, dropping down beside her as she gathered her legs up, smoothed her skirt, and wrapped her slender arms around her knees.

They sat there saying nothing for the longest time,

close enough that their shoulders brushed whenever either of them shifted so much as an inch. As the silent moments passed, Sin found that an answering stillness was growing inside him. He welcomed that stillness. After what had happened in the house and in the oak grove, that stillness felt cool and clean as the creek water sliding past at their feet.

Finally she said softly, "This spot appeared two years ago."

He looked at her, wondering what exactly she meant.

She told him. "We had a wet winter. The creek changed course. In the spring, this beautiful little glen was here."

He almost said, *No, it was here before. Right here. When I was little.* But he held the words back. Clearly the spot he'd loved as a child had been washed out years ago. This one was a new one, in just about the same place. No big mystery. Just an eerie coincidence.

She nudged him lightly with her shoulder, then asked in a shy voice that thoroughly captivated him, "Do you like it?" He looked at her directly as he had not dared to do since he'd forced his kiss and the knowledge of his desire on her, back in the shadowy grove of oaks.

She asked again, "Do you like it?"

"Yes. I do. Very much."

She let out a breath, a sigh that seemed to come not only from her, but from all around them—from the whispering willows, the gleaming creek and the tall pines, as well. "I knew that you would. I'll bet when you were little, you had a spot of your own, along this creek." A lock of that honey-colored hair lay curled on her shoulder. He couldn't resist touching it, smoothing it into the mass of thick waves that flowed down her back.

"Sinclair?" she prompted, her eyes bright as twin Sierra stars.

"Hmm?"

"Did you have a spot you called your own along this creek?"

"I might have."

She faked an injured look. "You're not going to tell me."

He touched her face, rubbed his thumb across her full lower lip. "No. I'm not." His body stirred again as her smile bloomed under his caressing thumb.

"It's all right. Keep your secrets."

"Thank you. I will."

Beneath his brushing thumb, her mouth felt like some ripe, ready fruit. He went on stroking it, back and forth, images flashing through his mind—the two of them, moving, naked, on the soft blanket of moss nearby; a big bed, with both of them in it, her skin like cream against snowy sheets.

Her eyes went lazy—with a desire that answered his own. And she canted toward him, closer, in a clear invitation to a kiss.

Sin wanted that kiss, the way a starving man wants bread.

And because he wanted it so badly, he refused to take it.

Inside his veins the blood pounded in hard heavy bursts. And still, he pulled his hand away and sat back a fraction.

She remained absolutely still for a moment. Then she made a little show of rearranging her skirts. He knew she was gathering herself back from the brink of the intimacy they hadn't quite shared.

He watched her compose herself, wondering why everything about her enchanted him, why he wanted to touch her so, when touching her should have been the last thing on his mind.

There *was* something about her. Something he couldn't turn away from, couldn't stop reaching toward—an innocence that beckoned. A goodness that lured.

Fool that he was, he did reach out again. He touched her white hem of cotton lace. "Your slip is showing."

She sat a little straighter. And then she stretched—an indolent movement that would have looked brazen on any woman but her.

Sin rubbed the soft, lacy fabric of her slip between his thumb and forefinger as she lifted her heavy hair with both hands and tipped her face toward the moon and the trees overhead. She smiled. Her throat gleamed, pale and perfect in the darkness, and her breasts pushed insolently against the supple fabric of her dress.

Watching her, Sin could feel his own natural restraint slipping inexorably away, like the water in the creek before them, so steadily and smoothly he could almost have told himself he didn't know that he would end up in her bed tonight.

But he did know. And in terms of his real goal, it was a mistake. In terms of his real goal, it would gain him nothing. Chances were, it would only make things all the messier later.

Sin Riker was a ruthless man. But even a ruthless man had his standards. It was one thing to check out his adversary, another altogether to climb into bed with her. For a man of his fastidious nature, having sex with people he intended to get rid of showed no discernment at all. It was simply a line he'd never crossed and never intended to cross.

But you will cross it now, a voice in his head taunted. *You will spend the night in her bed—and she will hate you later when she learns exactly what secrets you've kept from her tonight.*

He released her hem as she let her hair drop, the bronze mass cascading in a curling tangle down her back. "It's not a slip, it's a petticoat," she informed him. "And it's supposed to show."

"A petticoat." The old-fashioned word charmed him.

"Yes."

"Women don't wear *petticoats* anymore."

"This woman does." As she spoke, she took his arm and laid it across her shoulders. She slid him a mischievous grin. "All right?"

"Fine with me."

She leaned closer to him, fitting herself against him as if she belonged there. It felt very good. Soothing. To have her body touching his from shoulder to hip.

They were quiet once more, until she let out a sigh, and he whispered, "What?"

"Nothing. Life." She found his free hand and twined her fingers with his. "And you. I feel so close to you. Is that crazy?"

"Definitely."

"I don't care."

"You should care."

Sophie registered the warning in his voice. She

lifted her head from his shoulder and looked at him again.

Something had happened to her back in the house and then among the dark oaks. Some...*sureness* had come over her, that nothing that occurred between her and this man would ever be wrong. That a bond existed between them, never-ending and unbreakable: he who'd lost this place so young and she who was entrusted with the care of it now.

Yes, it was corny. And outrageously, impossibly romantic. And to Sophie B. Jones, that was just fine.

She lifted his hand and pressed it to her lips. "You feel it, too." He started to speak. She shook her head. "Don't."

"What?"

"Don't say you don't feel it. Don't tell a lie like that."

He said nothing. He was thinking of his other lies, though she couldn't know that.

She whispered, "And we *do* know each other." Now she guided their twined hands to her heart. "Here. Where it counts."

Sin could feel her heartbeat, feel the firm slope of her breast.

And her face was turned up to him, once more offering a kiss.

This time he couldn't resist. He moved closer. And so did she. Their lips touched so lightly.

It wasn't enough.

Not near enough.

He wanted more. He would *have* more.

With a low, hungry moan, Sin settled his mouth over hers.

Chapter Four

Warmth and life and breath made flesh, she melted into him. The scent of her surrounded him. Her soft lips gave beneath his, opening like some night-blooming flower to let him inside.

He took what she so freely offered, pressing her back against the dark rock they sat on, pulling her up even closer to him, so he could feel her slim body all along his as he plundered the sweetness beyond her parted lips.

But the rock was no good as a lovers' bed. Finally he had to end the kiss before they rolled off into the creek below. With a low groan of regret, he pulled away and looked down at her.

Her brown-and-gold hair spilled across the rough rock and her face, in the darkness, glowed like some rare pale flower. Her eyelids fluttered open and she stared back at him, giving him a mirror of his own yearning—as well as her absolute trust.

Trust he would ultimately demolish.

"I live in the guest house, did I tell you?"

He nodded.

"Come there with me now."

His body ached for the pleasure and release she would bring him. Yet, somewhere, far back in his mind, a stern voice commanded, *Stop now, walk away. Or give her the truth.*

"Sinclair. Come with me." She lifted a hand and laid it on the side of his face. He turned toward that hand. She sighed when he kissed the tender heart of her palm. "Come with me," she murmured again.

He opened his mouth, put his tongue out, tasted her flesh. She whispered his name on a moan.

He clasped her waist, and then higher, until he encompassed the soft globe of her breast.

"Now, Sinclair." She grasped his shoulder, the touch urgent and needful. "Let's go now."

He lowered his mouth to hers once more, stopping just short of the kiss they both craved.

"Sinclair." She used his name as a plea.

"Yes," he said against her parted lips. "Yes. Let's go. Now."

She led him along the creek again, and through the open field and the grove of oaks, then across the back lawn, through a rose arbor gate, to the small wood-frame house a hundred yards from Riker cottage.

He recalled that house vaguely. For a while, when he was very small, his grandmother Bernadette had lived there. It held only good memories for him. With no feelings of uneasiness at all, he stepped over the threshold into the small living room.

"I'll turn on some lights," she told him breathlessly.

She left him standing near the door as she went to flick on a Tiffany-style standing lamp in a corner. The warm light spread over the room, showing him fat, comfortable chairs, a sofa upholstered with twining vines and flowers, and tables that looked like antiques, though none of them matched. Before the lace-curtained front window stood a big Boston fern in a Chinese pot painted with rearing dragons.

On the walls were a number of pictures she must have picked up from estate sales or at flea markets, charming old-fashioned country scenes and a series of Victorian-looking prints. In one print, a turn-of-the-century lady sat at a writing desk, staring off into the middle distance as she composed her next line. In another, a man and a woman sat across from each other on twin love seats, sharing a coy look. And in a third, three golden-haired children picked flowers in a lush garden.

All the individual pieces were different than the ones his grandmother had owned. But it still felt exactly the same. Inviting. Comforting. Cozy. Warm.

"Hopelessly quaint, I know," Sophie said softly, still standing there by that Tiffany lamp.

He let himself look at her again. "I like it." And he did. Which was just more insanity. His house in the Hollywood Hills was all clean lines, light woods and floor-to-ceiling windows. Thoroughly modernist, with no clutter at all. A monk's mansion, Willa had called it. And maybe it was. As a grown man, there had been no appeal for him in Victorian prints and overstuffed furniture.

Until tonight…

"Well." Sophie brushed her hands nervously against the front of her skirt. "I'm glad. That you like it." Though a smile tilted the corners of her mouth, he could see the apprehension in her eyes.

He understood. Out there by the creek, under the spell of the night, making love with a stranger had seemed like just the right thing to do. But this wasn't a woman who gave her body to strangers. And now that they were actually here in her private space, her real nature had resurfaced. She couldn't keep the doubts at bay.

Which was good, Sin told himself. Looked at logically, it was the best thing that could have happened—so why did he feel this sharp pang of regret?

Hesitantly she moved toward him, stopping a few feet away, on the other side of that huge Boston fern. "I…my bedroom's that way." She gave a quick, awkward toss of one hand, toward the arch beyond her shoulder. He let his gaze follow the gesture, then looked at her once more.

She gulped. "Well. Shall we…?"

Slowly he shook his head.

Bewilderment clouded her beautiful eyes. "No?"

"Sophie. You're not ready for this." *And neither am I, for that matter.*

She took in a breath and let it out slowly. "Yes. I am. I…"

"Listen."

"What?"

"Just be a little practical. Think about safety. Think about…pregnancy."

Her face went red to the roots of her shining hair. "Pregnancy." She whispered the word.

Bluntness would be the kindest course. He took it. "Do you have contraception? Because I sure as hell don't."

"Oh." She gulped again. "I'm not...I didn't even think..."

"I know. Neither did I. Until right now."

She pressed her lips together, embarrassed, confused. She looked absolutely gorgeous to him in her indecision. He found he was becoming aroused all over again.

Best to get out. Now. "Look. It's been... beautiful." He allowed himself a grin. "And awful."

She actually smiled back. And then her eyes turned sad. "You're going."

"Yes."

"But...*where?*" Her honest face was so easy to read. She'd just realized she knew next to nothing about him. Nothing but his name, his distant past— the feel of his mouth on hers. "Um...where are you staying?"

He named his hotel in nearby Grass Valley.

"How...how long are you staying there?"

He shrugged. "I can't say for sure. I have some business to take care of. I'll be here till it's handled." *Which will be as soon as I can send you on your way.*

"I see." She dragged in another long breath and squared her slim shoulders. "Will you come back? Please? Tomorrow night. I'm free, same time as tonight, after the movie's over."

He nodded. He would come back, all right. And he would have himself thoroughly under control. He'd get things straight with her. Explain that he was her new landlord—and he wanted her out. He'd make her his offer. She would take it or not.

And that would be that. She would leave—or he would be forced to move to plan two.

Either way, this thing between them would be finished, which was good. It never should have gotten started in the first place.

"Around ten?" she asked so hopefully. "The show ends around ten."

His conscience, rusty and rarely used, prodded at him: Why put it off? Why not tell her right now?

He opened his mouth to do it. But all that came out was, "Fine. I'll see you at ten tomorrow night."

Sophie barely slept a wink that night. What had happened between herself and Sinclair almost didn't seem real, now he was gone and she lay all alone in her bed.

Really, she hardly knew a thing about him. He hadn't mentioned what he did for a living. Or how long he'd be staying in Grass Valley, or where he would go when he returned to wherever he now called home.

If he didn't come back tomorrow night as he'd promised, the only way she could find him would be to visit that hotel he'd mentioned. And if he'd checked out, she might never see him again.

But then, it was silly for her to think that way.

Of course, he'd come back. He'd said that he would. And tomorrow night, she vowed to herself, when they were alone again, she'd learn more about him.

She'd also make sure she was better prepared to go where her heart led her. True, she had a full day tomorrow. At this time of year, there was always more work to do than hours in the day. But inevitably, Myra would send her to pick up a few things. She could buy what she needed while she was out.

He didn't come to the movie.

Sophie sold the tickets from the small booth Caleb had made for her, right outside the barn doors. As each of her guests appeared out of the trees, coming from the small graveled area she'd designated as a parking lot, her heart rose—only to fall when she saw it wasn't him. By the time she'd closed the doors, shut the curtain from the entrance and concession area, and moved down in front to begin her introduction, she felt utterly bereft.

Which was so silly.

She'd told him to come *after* the movie—which he *had* seen just last night. There was no reason in the world for him to show up before ten.

Except that she *wanted* him to. And though she knew it was totally irrational, she kept feeling in her heart that he should know and respond to the longing she felt, that he should feel it, too, and be incapable of staying away.

Since he hadn't appeared before the show, she started hoping that he might come during intermission. She knew just how it should go: he would walk in, and she would hand him a bowl of popcorn and a bottle of spring water. She would look in his eyes and see a yearning so powerful—a longing every bit as overwhelming as her own.

"I saved a seat for you," she would say, her voice low and intimate, only for him.

He would give her one of those looks of his, a look

that meant to be distant—yet couldn't help being tender. "Thanks for the popcorn," he would murmur teasingly.

"You can help me wash the bowl later."

He would chuckle and head for the seat she'd saved him in the fifth row.

Through the whole of intermission, she kept expecting to look up and find him there, waiting to be handed his water and popcorn. But it never happened because he didn't come.

The show ended at ten o'clock. When she pushed open the doors, she just knew he'd be waiting on the other side, with the pines and the moon, the night breeze and the stars.

He wasn't.

She forced goodbye smiles for her guests. By ten-fifteen they had all disappeared back through the trees toward the parking lot, except for the few who needed a place to spread their sleeping bags for the night. She sent them off to the campground.

And then, all alone, she trudged back inside.

He wasn't coming. She was certain of it now. Tomorrow, she'd have to reach some sort of decision. Should she risk making a complete fool of herself trying to track him down? Or just set her mind to forgetting him?

Overhead, in the rafters, that pigeon she could never quite shoo out of there set to cooing. Sophie thought she'd never heard such a sad, lonely sound.

She looked at the stacks of empty popcorn bowls and thought of how Sinclair should have been here, offering, as he had last night, to help with the cleaning up. She kept remembering the way it had been last night, the two of them, in the little space in back, leaning against the sink, flirting, getting to know each other a little.

She couldn't face those bowls right now. It was just too depressing.

She cleaned up behind the concession counter, then moved on to the rows of seats, gathering up the few empty drink containers that the occasional thoughtless guest inevitably dropped on the floor. She got the broom and swept up, and finally carried the trash out to the big industrial-size bin around back.

By then, it was nearly eleven. And the popcorn bowls were still waiting.

With a sigh, Sophie scooped up half of them and carried them through the curtain to the sink. She had squirted in the dish soap and started the water running when that low velvety voice spoke from behind her.

"Let me make myself useful."

A warm shiver passed through her and her heart rose up. Suddenly she felt light as a white cloud in a clear summer sky.

But she didn't turn. Oh, no. After what he'd put her through, he didn't deserve to know he had her full attention—not yet, anyway. He came up on her left side, carrying the rest of the bowls. She edged to the right. The bowls in his hands tumbled into the sink. She watched the soap bubbles rising up beneath the stream of water.

She started washing, still not looking at him. "You're late."

He moved around her, to the other side of the sink. "No, I'm not." Turning the faucet his way, he started to rinse.

"I said ten o'clock."

"But I've been here since before the show started."

She dared a quick glance at him. Tonight, he wore a blue shirt and dark slacks. And he was every bit as fine as she remembered. He stole her breath and made her heart do flip-flops. "Here? At the Mountain Star?"

He nodded. "Down by the creek." *Thinking of your eyes. Wanting only to see you.* Dreading *what I have to say to you.*

Sophie picked up another bowl, swirled it in the soap suds and passed it to him. She felt as if she might laugh out loud—or burst into tears. Yet she strove for lightness, and somehow found it. "Afraid to face me, huh?"

You don't know the half of it. "Could be." He rinsed the bowl, set it to dry. "Caleb finally found me there."

"By the creek, in *our* spot?"

He looked at her then, a look of heat and longing, a look that made a day of agonized waiting worth it, after all. He turned off the water. Without that soft, rushing sound, the small space seemed to echo.

Into that echo, he asked, "You think of it as *our* spot now?"

"I do."

He lifted his wet hand and put his finger beneath her chin. She felt that touch all the way down to the absolute center of her being.

"What...were you doing there?"

"Nothing. Just sitting." He tipped up her chin. "Eventually Caleb found me there. He wanted to know what I was up to. I told him I was only sitting. Enjoying the creek and the trees. He let out a grunt, as if he didn't believe a word I'd said. And then he walked off and left me alone.''

''You said it yourself. He's protective of me.''

Sinclair moved his hand upward, so he cradled the side of her face. Sophie felt all quivery and warm—full of hope. And delicious desire. She did what he had done the night before, turning her face just enough that she could touch the soft inner pad at the base of his thumb with her lips. Water still clung there. She put out her tongue and licked it away.

He said her name, low and rough. ''Sophie.'' It sounded like a warning as well as a plea.

Though only a few of the bowls had been washed, she reached for a towel, dried her hands and passed the towel to him. He used it, then hung it back on its peg.

Before he could lower his hand, she caught it, cradled it, then smoothed the fingers open, so she could stroke his palm. ''I thought you weren't coming. It was awful. Never do that to me. Please. Never again.''

''Sophie…''

She looked up into his eyes.

He muttered roughly, ''We can't…''

She did not waver. She kept looking right into his eyes. ''Yes. We can. And we will.''

''You don't know…'' He let the words trail off.

''What?''

Now, he wouldn't meet her eyes.

She touched his jaw and guided his face around so he had to look at her again. ''Tell me. You can say anything to me. Anything at all.''

But he said nothing.

Somewhere nearby, just beyond the curtain to the

concession area, that pigeon started cooing again. They both turned toward the sound, and then back to each other.

He said her name again, low and rough, the same as before, "Sophie."

She only said, "Yes."

And then he reached out.

She went into his arms, joyous, eager, offering up her mouth.

And he didn't refuse her. He didn't try to argue with her anymore.

He only put his lips on hers and wrapped his arms around her, pulling her close and hard against him.

Heat and need shot through her, swirled around, moved out to the surface of her skin and then flowed back in again. And he went on kissing her, endlessly, only stopping once—to lift his mouth and slant it the other way.

Finally, with a joyous, breathless laugh, she pulled away. He made a sound, a needful moan deep in his throat, and tried to pull her back.

She resisted, moving away another step. "Come on. Let's go."

"Go where?" he demanded hoarsely.

"The guest house."

He stared. He looked stricken. Almost guilty. So strange.

"Sinclair? What is it?"

And then he was reaching for her, yanking her close again, kissing her some more. She sighed in delicious surrender, wrapping her arms around him, letting him have what he demanded of her, pressing herself close.

That time, he was the one who broke the kiss. He

tucked her head beneath his chin and held her so cherishingly, rocking from side to side a little, leaning back against the sink.

"You're too trusting," he whispered into her hair.

"No. This is right. You and me. This is…meant to be."

"Too damn trusting…" he muttered again.

She looked up, sought his eyes. "Is there someone else? Is that it?"

His brows drew together. "Someone else?"

"Another woman. A wife? A fiancée? A…live-in lover? Whatever."

He shook his head. "No one. Not anymore."

"Not…anymore?"

"There was someone," he admitted. "It didn't work out."

"What was her name?"

"Willa."

"Are you…still in love with her?"

"Love?" He was frowning.

"Yes. Love. Are you still in love with her?" Breath held, she waited for his answer, feared it wouldn't come.

But it did, at last.

"No. No, I'm not in love with her."

The surge of relief Sophie felt made her realize how afraid she'd been to ask those particular questions. "I'm so glad," she whispered. "So very, very glad."

He dragged in a breath. "Sophie—"

She didn't let him get any further. "I just want to *be* with you. Maybe it's not logical. Maybe it's not even wise. But it is right. I know it. It's the rightest thing in the world."

He only said her name again. She could see how much he wanted her, it was shining in those black eyes. So she lifted on tiptoe and pressed a quick kiss on his beautiful mouth. "Come with me. Now."

"Sophie, I—"

She stepped back. "I'm going to the guest house. And this time, I am *prepared*." By some miracle, when she said that, she managed not to blush. "Are you coming?"

He neither moved nor spoke. For an awful minute, she was sure he would say no.

But then, at last, he nodded.

She let herself breathe again. And she held out her hand.

Chapter Five

Her bedroom was like her living room: charming and old-fashioned. She had a big high bed with a carved headboard. A three-mirrored vanity. A heavy, bow-fronted bureau. Lacy curtains. Ferns.

Sin looked around him, wondering how the hell he'd gotten there, thinking that there was no excuse, by his own hard and cold rules of who he was and how he operated, for him to be there.

Yet he made no move to leave. Because he wanted her, a desperate kind of wanting that made no logical sense at all. And because she wanted him in return.

Last night her doubts had saved them both.

But not tonight. Tonight, the light of certainty shone in her eyes. Tonight, there would be no one saved. Tonight, she was ready. The conviction in her eyes held him. It beckoned him.

Goodness that lured.

She had the box of contraceptives waiting, right there by the bed. She gave him a sweet, rueful smile. "See?" she whispered. *"Prepared…"*

He grabbed her then, and started kissing her again—hard hungry kisses. She sighed and kissed him right back, turning cruelty to sweetness.

Baffled, bewildered, aching with want, he fell across that big old bed with her in his arms.

And then it was all awkwardness, all rolling and sighing and pulling at buttons, tugging at sleeves. Within moments, they were both naked, their clothes strewn beneath them, more softness on that soft bed.

Her sweet hands caressed him, her body called to his, a call he could neither deny nor refute.

They fumbled together with the box on the side of the bed. He rose above her. And then he was in her.

They both sighed. She looked up at him through those shining, trusting eyes.

Fast, it was. And needful. Without wariness. Or foreplay. Like no sex he'd ever known.

He kissed her on her white throat, latching on, sucking, and then moving lower to her full waiting breasts. She held him close against her heart, a heart that beat so strong and steady and sure.

By then, somehow time had slowed. Everything. Slowed. They moved together, rising and falling, connected, sharing pleasure. Sharing breath.

He remembered the stars last night. Running with her beneath the moon. The bed of green moss. The creek flowing on, forever, in that place that had been his. That place that shouldn't even exist anymore.

Yet it did exist. And it had become *theirs*. She had said so.

She said his name. His whole name. "Sinclair.…"

He lifted his head and looked down into her stunned, sweet face as her pleasure crested. Her body contracted around him, beckoning, urging.

He surrendered and joined her, pressing hard. Holding. Forever. Throwing his head back in a silent cry as his release finally took him down.

She moved in his arms, her gentle hand straying up to touch his brow. "Are you okay?"

He made a sound in the affirmative.

She sighed. "I'm glad."

He stroked her arm. "How about you?"

"I'm okay, too. Very much okay."

"Good."

She brought her sweet mouth closer. And he couldn't resist kissing her. She sighed some more, every smooth, supple inch of her eager and warm, soft. So fine and good.

"Oh!" she said into his mouth. She could feel him against her, wanting her. "Oh…"

He combed his fingers through the warm silk of her hair as the miracle began all over again.

All through that night, he kept thinking—whenever he *could* think—that this would be all of it, that he would somehow get enough of her. That after this, it would end.

But it didn't seem to be happening the way he kept thinking. Each touch only served to make the hunger stronger. Each release became a prologue to a kiss.

The smooth terrain of her body beguiled him. His hands and his mouth wandered everywhere. And she welcomed each separate, yearning caress.

Sometime near dawn, they finally slept.

He woke before her. It couldn't have been that

much later than when they'd dropped off. His mind felt clear and sharp as a cloudless winter sky.

He thought, I will wake her now. And somehow, I'll tell her—

But then she stirred. "Sinclair?" The word in his ear on a sweet exhaled breath.

And he was lost. He told her nothing. Only reached out and put his hand on her smooth belly.

She let out a small cry—of surprise and delight.

He moved his hand down.

"What do you do?" Her head rested on his arm and her legs were twined with his. "For a living?"

Carefully he told her, "I'm in property acquisition."

She moved beneath the sheet, untangling her legs from his, lifting up on an elbow. "Real estate? You buy and sell property?"

"Yes. For development mostly. Shopping malls. Office complexes."

"You said the other night that you had business to take care of. Are you planning to buy property here in Nevada County."

"Possibly. I'm…looking into the situation."

A coiling lock of hair fell over her eye. She blew it away. "Where do you come from?"

He stalled, saying nothing, trying to decide just how much to reveal.

She leaned in closer and pitched her voice to a teasingly conspiratorial level. "I'm asking you where you live."

He gave her the truth. "Los Angeles."

She grinned, flipped to her stomach and punched at her pillow. "There. That wasn't so hard, was it?"

She turned to her back, laced her hands behind her head and beamed at the antique light fixture overhead.

The fine bow of her collarbone tempted him. He indulged himself, moving close enough that he could run a finger from one shoulder to the other across the ridge of that bow.

She rolled her head to look at him. "Was it?"

"What?"

"Was it so hard?"

"No," he lied. "Not at all."

"You don't like to talk about yourself." Her tone had grown serious.

Again, he thought of what he should tell her—at the same time as he finally admitted to himself that he was not going to tell her. Not for a while yet.

He felt like a man under some sort of spell. A spell destined to end badly.

And soon.

But he would take what he could get while it lasted.

She said, "It's all right. I'll get the truth out of you." Now she looked mischievous. "One little bit at a time." She sat up. "How about a ride? Before breakfast."

"A ride?"

"You know. On a horse." She tipped her head. "Or maybe you don't ride."

"I ride. When I get the chance." It was part of his plan, to raise horses here. As his father had done and his grandfather before him.

She gave a small laugh. "How well? Can I vouch for you with Caleb?"

"You can vouch for me."

The sheet she held at her breast slid down, exposing the upper edge of one pink aureole. If she didn't get moving soon, he wouldn't let her go at all.

She must have seen the heat in his eyes. Her mouth went soft and her own eyes went dreamy. "I'm the general jane-of-all-work around here."

"So?"

"So, if we don't go for that ride now, we won't have time to go at all."

He reached for her, and the sheet fell away.

She sighed as he kissed her. "Maybe tomorrow morning…"

He lifted his mouth from hers, just enough to whisper, "Maybe tomorrow morning, what?"

"Maybe tomorrow morning, we'll go riding…." Smiling that dreamy smile, she pulled him down.

"Sinclair Riker." Myra said, as she set a roast beef sandwich and a big glass of milk in front of Sophie. "I can hardly believe it. And he's come back to see what became of his home?"

"Yep. And to look into doing business here, I think." Sophie picked up the sandwich. "This looks great. I am starving." She took a hefty bite. "Umm."

Myra watched her chew for a moment, then pulled out the chair opposite her and sat in it. Sophie cast her a questioning glance. The older woman poked a loose strand of graying red hair back into the net she wore when she worked, then moved the salt and pepper shakers closer together in the middle of the table.

Sophie swallowed the bite of sandwich. "Okay. What's up?"

They were alone in the kitchen, but still the cook leaned forward and lowered her voice. "He spent the night, didn't he?"

Sophie swallowed. "Myra," she said gently. "You are not my mother."

Myra sat back in her chair and crossed her freckled arms over her middle. "Well, of course, I'm not."

"And anyway, how would you know if he spent the night?"

Myra uncrossed her arms and looked at the table. She must have spied a few crumbs, because she began blotting the table with her fingers. "Caleb ran into him down by the creek last night—and then saw him leave this morning."

"And naturally Caleb reported right to you."

"You know how he is." The cook rubbed her fingers together over her other hand, then blotted the table some more. "He just wants to protect you."

"I don't need protecting. Honestly."

"But…" Myra seemed unable to find the right words. She stood, went to the sink, and brushed away the crumbs she'd blotted up. Then she turned back to Sophie. "It's only…you just met him, right?"

Sophie set down her sandwich. She pushed back her chair and went to stand beside the older woman. Myra had come to the Mountain Star in response to Sophie's ad for a live-in cook. She'd been the first applicant for the job. Myra had worked in restaurants, both at the stove and as a waitress. Her references had been impeccable. But more important to Sophie, Myra had kind eyes. Sophie had just known that they would be great friends. And she had been right.

"Myra, remember how you used to worry, when we first started out? When we opened the campground and people who needed somewhere to spend the night began showing up?"

Myra made an obstinate noise in her throat. "That was different."

"No. I don't think so. You were worried that one of them might cause us harm. But none of them have. It's all worked out fine."

"They're good kids, most of them. I see that now."

"Myra, you give them food. To take with them when they go."

"Only leftovers, you know that. In order not to waste them. And you did tell me to use my judgment about it."

"That's right. Because I trust your judgment."

"Well," Myra muttered grudgingly. "Thank you."

"And now, I would like for you to trust mine."

Myra's gaze skittered away. "Of course, I trust your judgment."

"Good."

"But...this is so unlike you."

"No." Sophie touched her friend, very lightly, on the shoulder. "It's exactly like me. Myra, I..." She couldn't quite say the word *love* at that point, though that was what she felt inside. Still, her relationship with Sinclair was all too new, too overwhelming, to go putting labels on it. She finished rather lamely, "I trust him. I do."

"But how do you know if he's a man worthy of trust? You don't even go *out* with men."

Sophie laughed then. "When would I have time? You know how it is around here. I barely manage to fit in a few hours' sleep at night." And last night, not even that much, she thought, and had to hide a goofy smile.

"Yes," Myra jumped in, "and that's what I mean.

You're not…experienced. You're not careful. You're a perfect target for some fast-talking fortune hunter.''

Sophie made a show of rolling her eyes. "Some fortune. We run this place on a shoestring, and you know it perfectly well. Sinclair knows it, too."

"How does he know?"

"Because he has eyes. Because I gave him a tour of this kitchen. All he had to do was glance around. He could see I don't have the money to fix it up right."

"Is that what he said?"

"Honestly, Myra. He's not after my *fortune*. I promise you."

"Then what is he after?"

Sophie pretended to be hurt. "What? You find it impossible to believe he might just be after *me?*"

"No." Myra's ruddy face lost its obdurate expression. "I don't find that impossible. You know I don't."

"Good. And I'm not a total innocent. I've been around a little—back before the Mountain Star, when I had a Saturday night to myself now and then."

"You've…been around?" The cook frowned.

Sophie immediately regretted her choice of words. "Oh, Myra. You know what I mean. There was a time when I actually dated. And I was engaged once, before I came here."

"That's right, I'd forgotten. That lawyer from San Francisco…"

"The point is, I'm not a complete fool when it comes to the opposite sex."

"Oh, I do hope you're right." The cook glanced at the rest of Sophie's sandwich, which still waited on the table. "You'd better eat that before the bread gets dry. And drink all that milk. The way you work, you need a good lunch.''

"Myra, are you all right about this now?''

Myra sniffed. "I don't approve of what you're doing.'' And then she couldn't help smiling. "But I do approve of *you*.'' She sighed. "I suppose it's your life.''

"Thank you. For caring.''

"Eat your lunch, then.''

"I will.''

After she finished her sandwich and drank all of her milk, Sophie went looking for Caleb. She found him in the stables, wearing those high rubber boots of his, swamping out stalls.

He looked up when he saw her, then went back to work.

"Caleb, I think we'd better talk.''

He went on pushing his broom. "Maybe later. I want to get this job done now.''

"Caleb.''

He stopped, glanced at her narrowly, then set the broom against the wall. "What?''

She found she didn't know how to begin. "Look. Let's go out to the big pasture.'' The big pasture was several hundred yards from the stables, to one side of the series of working corrals. The horses whose owners hadn't come to claim them for the day would all be there now.

"Sophie B., I got my work to do.''

"It won't take long. I promise.''

Reluctantly he followed after her, out into the sunlight. They leaned on the fence of the pasture and watched the horses. The big spotted gelding Pretty

Boy came over, lipped Sophie's empty palm, then ambled away.

Sophie watched him go. ''Sinclair is welcome here, Caleb,'' she said softly. ''I...care for him.''

Beside her, Caleb grunted, a disapproving sound.

''Caleb, I know what I'm doing.''

Caleb grunted again.

''Give him a chance.'' She reached out, put a hand on his huge forearm. ''For my sake.''

He actually looked at her then. ''You think you know what you're doing?''

She nodded. ''I *do* know what I'm doing. I'm sure. In my heart, where it counts.''

''It's happened pretty sudden.''

''Things that happen suddenly aren't necessarily bad.''

He actually smiled then, something he did rarely, because his teeth were crooked and that embarrassed him. ''I guess you got a point. I like things slow, myself. But that's maybe just me.''

''Sometimes you simply have to be ready. Or the best things in life will pass you by.''

Caleb turned back to the horses again. ''The vet said Black Angel's doing fine.'' The Arabian mare had come up lame a few weeks ago. A bad sprain, but not a break, thank heaven. The owner had had a fit, though both Sophie and Caleb knew the limp had started right after the woman had taken the mare out for a long ride on the twisting trails of Riker Ranch. Caleb had suffered the owner's abuse, then wrapped the injured pastern joint, stalled the horse and called in the vet.

''She looks good as new,'' Sophie said.

Caleb turned his pale blue eyes on her again. ''I

guess if you think this Sinclair Riker's okay, it's good enough for me.''

Sophie touched his arm again. ''That's what I hoped you'd say.''

''He just better treat you right, that's all.''

''Oh, Caleb. He's a fine man.''

''If you say so.''

''I do.''

That night, Sinclair arrived at intermission. Sophie looked up and saw him. He smiled. She almost dropped a can of grape soda on a guest's sandaled foot.

''Careful, Sophie B.,'' the guest warned.

She apologized, handed the guest his change and waited on the next person in line—a true exercise in concentration since every atom in her body seemed to be bouncing around in pure joy.

Finally everyone had been served. Sinclair straightened from the little table by the door, where he'd been leaning, watching her. In three long strides he stood before her.

She looked up at him, feeling stunned and glorious. Out of her depth, over her head—and thrilled to be that way. ''Hi.''

''Hello.''

''Popcorn? Bottled water?''

He shook his head. ''Not tonight.''

''Oh.'' She felt at a loss, all at once, like an actress who had forgotten her next line. ''Will you...watch the rest of the show?''

''I think I'll pass. Those poor evil rustlers. I can't stand to see them all die a second time.'' He was teasing her.

By some minor miracle, she found she could tease back. "They deserved to die. They crossed Randi Wilding."

"Who looks damn good in a tight plaid shirt."

She put on a reproachful expression. "Randi Wilding is more than a sex symbol. She is a genius on film."

"I still think I'll pass up the second half."

"And do what?"

"Go for a walk—if that's all right."

"You know it is."

His mouth twisted wryly. "Maybe you should give me a grounds pass. Something that says it's all right if I'm here—in case I run into Caleb."

"Caleb won't bother you. He knows you're okay now."

His eyes gleamed. "And how does he know that?"

"Because I told him."

"And how do *you* know that?"

"I have my ways." She glanced toward the curtain that led to the rows of seats. All her guests were waiting to see the second half. "And I also have to get that projector going."

"I know."

Neither of them moved.

"Sinclair, I really have to go."

He reached out and slid his hand under her hair, cupping the back of her neck and pulling her close. "I know," he said again. And then he kissed her.

Oh, had there ever been such kisses as his? They seared her synapses. Sent her eyeballs spinning...

When he let her go and stepped back, she swayed toward him, like a green tree in a high wind. He laughed then. "Just so you won't forget me."

"As if I ever could."

"Go on. Your audience wants to see the rest of the show."

Somehow she made her feet turn toward the hayloft.

Afterward he was waiting. He helped her wash the bowls and sweep the floor. Then they went to the guest house together.

They were barely through the front door before he was grabbing her, pulling her close, kissing her as if he might die if he didn't. She kissed him back. She felt just the same way—as if she must kiss him, or she wouldn't survive.

They took off all their clothes and lay down on the couch.

The things they did there should have made her blush for shame.

But she didn't blush. And she felt no shame. She felt only rightness.

And pure ecstasy.

Those beautiful hands moved over her, revealing all her secrets, making her cry out. Making her moan. She lifted herself up to him, offering herself, welcoming whatever glorious anguish his next caress might bring.

Finally he said, "The bedroom. Now."

He got up and took her hand and tugged her along, totally naked, dazed, yearning, fulfilled and yet still hungry, into the other room. He let go of her hand just inside the door and she stood there, watching him, as he moved toward the bed. His body glowed in the darkness, lean and hard, the muscles spare and tightly sculpted. So beautifully formed. So perfectly male.

As she looked at him, she wondered at herself.

"This isn't like you," Myra had said.

And it wasn't.

Or rather, it hadn't been. Until Sinclair.

And now she couldn't get enough of this. Of him. Of his body. Her body. The two of them. Joined.

He found the box of contraceptives, took one out, rolled it down over himself. And then he turned. "Come here."

The yearning inside her rose up, hotter than ever, to meet the command in his voice. In his burning dark eyes. There was a thrumming all through her, a rhythm of pure need.

She moved toward him. He sat on the edge of the bed, held out his hand. She took it. He pulled her onto his lap, there on the edge of the bed.

She settled over him, gasping a little at the torrent of pure feeling as he filled her. He guided her legs around her hips and his mouth found her throat in a long, hungry kiss. She closed her eyes, let her head fall back.

Heaven. A forbidden heaven, it was. She soared through it, her whole body shimmering. Joyous. Free.

Finally, near the end, she made herself open her eyes and look at him.

He stared back at her, a look as deep and powerful as the uproar in her blood.

She whispered, "I love you. Love you, love you…"

The fulfillment came. Hard and fast. Her head fell back again. She left all conscious thought behind as sensation had its way with her.

Chapter Six

Right at daylight, she shook him and called his name.

He put an arm over his eyes and groaned.

"Sinclair, I want you to go riding with me."

He sneaked a glance out from under his arm. Her hair hung over her bare shoulders, glorious and tangled. She looked like some sleepy angel—a frowning angel.

"What's the matter?" He lowered his arm.

"I just realized that you don't have riding clothes."

He grinned at her. "I do. In the car."

"You do?" Now she was beaming, happy as a good child on Christmas Eve.

"You said you wanted to ride this morning, so I brought some jeans and boots."

She yanked back the sheet. "Well, don't just lie there. Get up. We have to get going. Come on..."

* * *

The hulking stableman didn't seem much friendlier, but he stayed out of the way as Sin and Sophie saddled up a pair of horses and got ready to go.

The sun was just sliding over the edge of the mountains when they started on the trail that wound off into the trees not far from the main house. She led the way through the pines and then out into a sunny, rolling pasture overgrown with tangled wild rosebushes. Soon enough, they went back into the trees again and then upward, switching back and forth toward the rocky crest of a high hill.

When they reached the top, they stopped and looked out over the blanket of evergreen below, broken up here and there by small meadows and the shining ribbons of mountain streams. Sin leaned on the saddle horn, thinking that the damn pines were choking out everything. They encroached on all the meadows now, saplings and even midsize pines dotting what had once been open land. Something would have to be done about them, or the ranch would be nothing but forest.

"Is it the same as you remember it?" she asked.

He let out a low laugh. "Sophie. I was only six." Yet he did remember. His father had brought him up here once, about a year before the end. To look out over the land, just as he and Sophie were doing now.

"All that you can see is ours," his father had said. "Riker land. Your grandfather scraped and saved and wheeled and dealed for every square foot of it. It's what makes us who we are."

Even now, over thirty years later, Sin felt his blood stir as he remembered his father's words. Anthony Riker had always been a hell of a talker. He could bring tears to the eyes of the coldest heart when he quoted poetry or told the old family tales.

Unfortunately he'd hated work and never planned ahead. Busy telling stories and quoting Browning and Shelley, he'd let the land that "made them who they were" slip right through his fingers. And then he'd killed himself, a final dramatic statement that also allowed him to escape a future in which he'd no longer be Anthony Riker of the Riker Ranch, but just another nobody trying to scrape by day-to-day.

Beside him, Sophie spoke. "It gives me such a feeling of…peace, just to look at it. To know that even with all the ugliness in the world, a place like this exists."

The brown gelding Sin rode snorted and tossed his head, eager to be moving again. Sin patted his neck to settle him down a little and set his mind on practical matters. "It's overgrown. A little clear-cutting would help." He used the logger's term for the removal of every last tree from any given area. Sophie sent him a sharp, disapproving glance. He laughed. "Come on. Clear-cutting has its uses, in spite of what your average rabid conservationist would like you to believe. Give it another twenty years, and those pines down there will choke out everything."

She looked out over the land, her angel's face wistful. "I suppose. But still, it's so beautiful and wild-looking."

"Overgrown," he reiterated grimly. Then he couldn't resist adding, "I'm surprised that teachers' association you mentioned didn't bring in some logging crews. The lumber would have brought them a little return on that 'bad investment' of theirs."

She made a face at him. "You'll be pleased to know that they did get some crews in here at first."

"But lately?"

"The past few years, the laws have become so much stricter. It's hard to get permits to cut trees, even on private land."

"Hard, but not impossible."

She smiled at him, a rather sad smile. "Maybe Inkerris, Incorporated, will put some loggers to work."

He only shrugged, though he knew damn well that Inkerris, Incorporated, planned to do exactly that.

She clucked her tongue at the mare she rode. "Come on. I have to get back."

He didn't argue, just turned his horse for the trail.

"Stay for Sunday brunch," she urged once they'd handed their horses over to Caleb. "It's buffet style. We put it out from ten to one. You could go back to the guest house and relax for a while, then wander on over and get something to eat."

The offer held definite appeal—except for the idea of entering that house again.

It was as if she read his mind. "You're uncomfortable about visiting the cottage again. I understand. Listen, I could load you up a plate and bring it back to the guest house and we could—"

He cut her off with a flat lie. "I'm not uncomfortable about that damn house."

She looked down at the pine needles under their feet. "Fine."

He dragged in a breath. "Look. I'm sorry. I spoke too harshly."

She shot him a glance. "So stay for brunch."

"No, I can't. I've got some work to do back at the

hotel.'' Another lie. His only job here was getting rid of her—a job that had not progressed at all as he'd planned.

She met his gaze again. And smiled. God, she could finish a man off with that smile. "You could go work for a few hours—and come back for brunch. I'd fix us each a plate and take it to the guest house.''

The word *yes,* was out of his mouth before it even took form in his brain.

At the hotel, he showered, checked his messages and called Rob Taylor, his personal assistant in LA, at home. Rob had a number of issues to report on. Sin listened with half an ear, made a few suggestions, then said he had to go.

By then, it was nine-thirty. Too soon for a man who had "work" to do to be showing up again at the Mountain Star. He checked at the front desk and got the name of a local health club that took drop-ins on Sunday, then he got in his rental car and drove over there.

He worked out for an hour, pushing his body until the sweat was streaming off of him and his muscles felt like limp spaghetti. When he couldn't press another pound, he showered for the second time that day.

He was on his way back to the Mountain Star when he noticed the gray sedan behind him. A late-model Plymouth or Dodge. So nondescript as to be almost invisible. But now that he thought about it, it seemed he'd seen more than a few late-model gray sedans in his rearview mirror the past day or two.

Right then, he was just leaving the part of Grass Valley known as the Brunswick Basin, a busy shopping area packed with strip malls, fast-food restaurants and gas stations. He swung into the next parking lot: home to a bank, a title company and a beauty parlor. The gray sedan sped on by. When Sin pulled back onto the road again, the car was nowhere in sight.

Through the remainder of the short drive to the ranch, he tried to think which of his current competitors or business associates might want him followed. No one came immediately to mind. But that didn't mean anything. He had a reputation for sealing up prime pieces of property before his potential rivals even realized that the property could be bought.

He'd left LA in the middle of last week. No doubt by now, the word would be out that he was gone. It was entirely possible that someone had had him followed just to see what fabulous deal he might have in the works.

Sin smiled to himself. If someone had had him followed, they should have done some spying a little closer to home first. Sin paid his people well and expected their discretion, but information could always be obtained at a price. An effective rival could have learned that the property in question already belonged to him—and that this was a purely private matter anyway.

Sin signaled, slowed down, and turned into the long driveway that led to the Mountain Star. He wasn't overly concerned—but nonetheless, he would remember to keep an eye out for nondescript sedans.

Sin and Sophie had their private brunch in the bedroom of the little house.

Afterward she couldn't linger. She had to get right back to work. Reluctant to return to his hotel where he would only sit and contemplate the sheer idiocy of his own behavior, Sin wandered out to the stables. There he found Caleb, the surly stableman, helping an angry-looking blonde onto the back of a coal black Arabian mare. The woman, who might have been anywhere from thirty to forty, wore English riding gear—jodhpurs, a neat little hat and knee-high boots. Once she found her seat, she sawed on the reins, forcing the mare to prance.

"Easy," Caleb warned.

The woman cast him an icy glance, yanked on the reins some more, and rode out into the sun as if she owned the world.

Shaking his head, Caleb watched her go. Then he turned and saw Sin standing there.

"That's a fine mare," Sin said.

"And that woman's set on ruining her," Caleb replied. He turned to leave.

Sin should have let him go, but instead he heard himself say, "Wait."

The big man turned. "Yeah?"

"How did you meet Sophie?"

Caleb broadened his stance a little—a pose that Sin read as wariness. "Why do you need to know?"

"I don't. I'm just curious."

A gray cat came strolling toward them across the red dirt in front of the stables. It looked like the same one Sophie had held in her arms that first night, while she gave her cute little introductory speech before the Randi Wilding Western. The cat ran up to Caleb, let out a meow and then sat back in a sinuous movement on its hind legs.

The stableman bent, scooped it up and began petting it in long strokes. The cat closed its eyes and purred in ecstasy. Caleb said, "She found me here."

"Sophie?"

Caleb nodded, his big head bent down, his gaze on the purring cat. "She came here by accident. She was living in the city then."

"The city? You mean San Francisco?"

"Yeah. She came up here for a weekend with a boyfriend."

Sin felt a completely irrational surge of jealousy. "A boyfriend."

"That's right. She was going to marry him."

"Why didn't she?"

Caleb looked up. "You'll have to ask her about that." He looked down at the cat again, went on stroking the gray fur. "She was alone when she came here, though."

"You mean to the ranch itself?"

"Uh-huh. Just drove up the driveway one day, curious, wanting to look around at the old Riker place. She found me in the barn. I was…camped out there. I had nowhere else to go." He raised his head, his pale eyes proud, defiant of any judgments Sin might make.

"You were homeless."

"That's what they call it." His gaze was on the cat again, stroking, rubbing. "She wasn't even scared of me. She's like that. She trusts. Everybody gets the benefit of the doubt with her." He shot another quick glance up at Sin. Sin caught the meaning of that glance: *Everybody gets the benefit of the doubt with her, even some who probably shouldn't, even you.…*

The cat rolled over in the groom's huge arms. He scratched its belly. "Anyway, she found me here. We started talking. I told her I loved horses, could fix just about anything with a motor, and knew what to do to bring the grounds back under control—everything was grown pretty wild by then. She always says she got the idea for the Mountain Star that day, with just her and me. Talking in the barn."

Sin decided to go for the throat. "You're in love with her."

Caleb crouched and let the cat down. It strolled away, tail high. Then slowly Caleb stood. He assumed that wide, guarded stance again. "I love her. But not the kind of love you think. I'd do anything for her. She's the sister I never had." He paused, looked at Sin sideways. "You ever had a sister?"

"No."

"A man feels protective of a sister. I suppose what I'm tellin' you is, I would do bad damage to a man who hurt her."

"I see."

"Good. And I got work to do."

Sin watched him walk away.

That night, as they lay in bed, Sin kept thinking of that other man, the one she had almost married.

And Sophie knew, the way she always did, that something was bothering him. "Okay, what is it?"

He went ahead and told her. "I spoke with Caleb today."

"He was civil—I hope?"

"Civil enough. He told me you were almost married once."

"That's true."

"What happened?"

Sophie thought, *he wasn't you,* but didn't say it.

She'd gone and cried out her love just last night, and he'd said nothing. She didn't want to push him with constant declarations of her feelings. To her, it seemed she'd been waiting all her life for him to come and find her. But in reality, this was only the fourth night since he'd walked into her movie theater and stolen her heart. She wanted him to feel free to open up to her in his own time and in his own way.

"Sophie?" His warm breath caressed her shoulder. "Tell me about him."

She didn't hesitate. She wanted him to know all about her own life, just as she hoped he would soon tell her more about his. "His name was David. He was a lawyer. Family law. He handled my aunt Sophie's estate—she was the one who raised me, really. My parents were killed in a car crash when I was only five.

"I met David when Aunt Sophie died. That was six years ago. I was twenty-one, with a degree from a business school and a job in an insurance office. I felt very grown-up. After we'd been dating for about six months, he asked me to marry him. He was a good man and I was...lonely. With Aunt Sophie gone, I had no family left. I said yes."

"And?"

"And then we came here. For a weekend. I went off by myself one day, exploring. I stopped at this coffee shop in Grass Valley and got talking to some of the old fellows at the counter. They told me a few stories. About the town."

He added for her, "And about the Rikers, who carved an empire here—and then lost it, all in the space of two generations?"

"Yes." She turned toward him, cuddled closer. "I

asked where the Riker Ranch was. They gave me directions and I found my way here. I drove up the entrance road and...fell in love.''

"With this place." It wasn't a question. He understood.

"Yes. I wanted to move here. To spend the money my aunt had left me to create the Mountain Star."

"And David didn't share your dream."

"He had his life in San Francisco and he didn't want to move." Sinclair's black hair had fallen over his forehead. Tenderly, Sophie combed it back with her fingers.

"Do you still think of him?"

"Sometimes. But not with regret. It just...wasn't meant to be."

He reached for her, cupped the back of her neck. "Lucky for me."

"Oh, Sinclair..."

"Kiss me."

She did.

For a good while, they didn't speak. The only sounds in the lace-curtained room were soft moans and sighs.

Later she gathered all her courage, and asked, "When did your mother die?"

He hesitated, but then he did answer. "About three years ago."

"Of what?"

"Complications from diabetes, the doctors said."

"You don't believe that?"

He moved away from her a little, and sat up against the carved headboard. "I believe she wanted to die. Diabetes can be managed, but she refused to take care of herself. She was never happy, in all those years after my father killed himself.''

She pulled the sheet against her breasts and sat up beside him. ''It must have been hard for you growing up, if she was unhappy.''

''We got by.'' The three words were like a wall with a sign on it: *Keep Out.*

Still, she pressed on. ''What did she do…for a living?''

He gave her a long, deep look. ''You don't want to know.''

She felt for his hand, twined her fingers with his. ''No, that's not true. I do want to know.''

''All right.'' He paused. She thought for a moment that he had changed his mind and wouldn't go on, but then he said, ''She lived off of men.''

Sophie hoped she hadn't heard right. ''Excuse me?''

Sinclair chuckled, a cold sound.

''You ought to see your face. You shouldn't have asked.''

She scooted over even closer to him, brought their twined hands to her heart. ''But I want to know, I do. Whatever you're willing to tell me.''

He looked at their clasped hands, then pulled his away. ''All right, Sophie. I'll tell you. She was a whore.''

''A…?'' She gulped, her throat closing over the ugly word.

''You heard me. A whore.''

''But I don't understand. You're saying she became a…prostitute? Just like that?''

He made a low, impatient sound. ''No. Not *just like that*. She drifted into it. She was a pretty woman and men were attracted to her. Like my father, she had little ambition to get out and make things happen. At first, I remember she had a job in an office. We lived in east Hollywood then, a tiny 'garden' apartment in a neighborhood that had gone downhill. The job didn't pay much. She was always late with the rent and always worried about how we would get by. And then she met someone at that office. I suppose you could say she was his mistress for a while. Then he dumped her and she lost the job. She met someone else. And someone else. Eventually, she stopped having affairs. She went out with men and went to bed with them and they paid her for it.

"She went on like that until I got old enough to do something about it. I bought her a little house in the San Fernando Valley and I took over paying her bills for her. She lived quietly after that, but she drank. Drinking and diabetes don't mix." He was looking at the far wall. "Three years ago, she died."

At last, he turned his gaze her way again. "Heard enough?"

She kept picturing him as a little boy, in that tiny apartment he'd mentioned—all alone, while his mother went out with strange men. "How did you stand it? How did you live?"

"Let's say I was determined."

"Determined to do what?"

Sin wondered what the hell was the matter with him, to have revealed so much.

"Sinclair."

"Umm?"

"What were you so determined to do?"

He backpedaled—smoothly, he hoped. "To... better myself, I guess you could say." He settled down onto the pillows and pulled her close. "You ought to get some sleep."

She wrapped one arm around him, twined those long, smooth legs with his. "Sinclair?"

"What?"

"I'm so sorry for her. And for you."

"Don't be," he commanded. "She's gone now. And I've got what I wanted."

She snuggled up closer. "You mean money, right?"

"Right," he lied in a whisper, "that's what I mean." He smoothed her shining hair back from her temple and placed a kiss there. "Now, go to sleep."

"Sinclair?"

"Sophie. Go to sleep."

She sighed. She had a thousand more questions, and he knew it. But he wasn't going to answer them. He'd already told her way too much.

She must have realized that he was through talking, because she said no more.

The next morning, right as the sun rose, she dragged him over to the cottage to eat breakfast in the kitchen with her and the help—which included Caleb, the cook named Myra and a skinny little part-time maid called Midge.

Sin still didn't care much for spending time in that house. One of the first things he intended to do once he took over was to tear the damn thing down and build again.

But that morning, with Sophie next to him, the old demons stayed away.

Midge was a talker. She had a boyfriend who kept leaving and then coming back, a mother who wouldn't quit giving her advice—and she'd flunked her last semester at Sierra Junior College.

"Oh, I dunno," Midge informed them all between big bites of scrambled egg, "I just dunno what to do. Maybe I should get a full-time job. Get my own place, not have to listen to Mother anymore. But then, higher education has always been my dream. Without a college degree, how will I ever really make something of myself?" She gulped down more egg and fluttered her skimpy lashes at Sin. "What do you think, Mr. Riker?"

He said something neutral.

She started babbling again.

The red-haired cook spoke up the next time Midge paused to shovel in more food. "So, how long will you be staying in town, Mr. Riker?"

Beside him, he felt Sophie go very still. She'd asked him that question herself once, the first night he came here. He had evaded. And she hadn't asked again.

"Mr. Riker?" the cook prompted, reminding him of a disapproving schoolmarm who'd waited too long for a response from a student she didn't much like anyway.

"I'll be here another week. Maybe two." Idiocy. Pure and simple. Things couldn't go on this way for another two weeks.

But even as he admitted the impossibility of the situation, he knew he planned to carry on with it—and with Sophie—for as long as the lie lasted.

"Sophie says you're here on business."

"Yes."

"And what kind of business is that?"

Sin caught the warning glance Sophie sent Myra's way, but Myra kept her sharp green eyes right on him.

"I'm in real-estate acquisition."

"You're buying property here, in Nevada County?"

"I'm…checking out the situation."

Caleb joined the interrogation then. "What does that mean?"

"Caleb, please." Sophie jumped to the rescue. "Sinclair is our guest."

Sin put his hand over hers. "It's all right." He looked at Caleb—and began dishing out more half truths. "What I mean is, before I would buy property here for potential development, I would have to thoroughly investigate the climate for such a project."

"The climate?"

"Would the community be open to it? Would local government stymie us at every turn—or make the thousand and one permits we'd need easy to acquire?"

"We don't want another shopping mall around here anyway," Caleb said sourly.

Now it was Myra's turn to shoot the big man a quelling look, after which she started in on Sin again. "So, you're here to find out if you want to do business in Nevada County. Is that it?"

"You could say that, yes." Though it wouldn't be true.

"And that could take two more weeks?"

"It could."

Right then, someone tapped on the door that led out to a small back porch. All heads turned that way. Sin knew a shameful moment of total relief, to have the inquisition over—at least for the moment.

Myra pushed back her chair. ''That'll be the campers.'' She went to the door.

Two thin, shabbily dressed older men stood there, bedrolls and packs slung over their shoulders. ''Good morning, Myra.'' One of them tipped the sweat-stained felt hat he wore.

''You just hold it right there.'' The cook bustled off toward the pantry.

The man in the felt hat caught sight of the rest of them and tipped his hat a second time. ''Howdy, folks—Sophie B.''

Sophie gave him one of those smiles of hers, a smile bright enough to light up the whole room. ''Hello, Edgar. And Silas, how are you?''

''Just fine, ma'am. Beautiful day.''

''Yes. It certainly is.''

''Come on in,'' Sophie said.

''No,'' the one called Edgar shook his head. ''We got to be going.''

Myra emerged from the pantry carrying two small brown paper sacks. ''Just a little something. It'll be lunchtime before you know it.''

''We surely do thank you, Myra.''

''That we do. A bite always comes in handy.''

''You boys take care of yourselves now.''

''You know we will....'' They went off down the walk and Myra closed the door. She returned to the table.

Sin looked at Sophie. ''Bag lunches for the homeless?''

Midge piped up again. ''Edgar and Silas aren't homeless. Well, not exactly, anyway. They're prospectors. They dredge the South Fork. But they never made a big strike. So they kind of ended up living day-to-day.''

Sin held back a chuckle over that one. His grandfather had worked in the mines, after all. And his father had been an expert on the history of the area.

Silas and Edgar had chosen the wrong business. Though some hard-rock mining concerns still operated in the gold country with reasonable success, no dredger he'd ever heard of had made a big strike in the past hundred years or so.

Midge went on. ''But they do drink, I heard—Edgar and Silas, I mean. They both got a liquor problem, like a lot of miners. It's sad. It comes from busted dreams, the way I see it. If you got no dreams left, you got to soothe yourself with something.''

Sin hardly heard her. He was looking at Sophie, remembering how it had irritated him the other night when she'd sent those kids out to sleep on his land. Today he felt differently. Today he felt... admiration. Yes, *admiration* was the word. Admiration for a woman who didn't have the money to put a decent kitchen in her rundown resort, but still let her cook pass out food to every down-and-outer who knocked on the back door.

Admiration.

It wasn't like him. Not like him at all.

Sophie smiled at him, reached for her coffee cup and drained the last of it.

Midge went on, ''But still, I gotta say, it might not be so bad. To live free in an old van like Silas and Edgar. And in the summertime, to sleep out under the stars. To have Myra give me bag lunches when I got really hungry. It might be better than *my* life, for instance.

"I mean, It's not easy, worrying every day about my GPA, listening to my mother nagging and wishing that my boyfriend would either ask me to marry him or get his sorry butt out of my life. I just—"

Myra had heard enough. "Finish up. I want some help to get the breakfast on in the dining room. And then you've got vacuuming and dusting and a freezer to defrost."

Midge let out a long, deep sigh. Then she picked up her fork and finished her second helping of scrambled eggs.

Chapter Seven

Sin left as soon as he'd finished his breakfast. After all, he had to keep up the fiction that he had lots of work to do, checking out the local business climate, courting the county politicos.

Sophie walked him to his car. They stopped on the path before they reached the parking area under the pines.

"The theater's closed tonight." She swayed a little closer to him, turning her face up, so her sweet mouth was only inches from his. "And tomorrow night. And the next night, too. I only run it Thursday through Sunday. Did I tell you that before?"

He looked at her slim nose and her wide mouth and those beautiful eyes. He was like some adolescent with his first crush—he just couldn't get enough of looking at her.

"Sinclair, did I tell you?"

"You might have."

"Well, anyway, now you know. That's three nights a week I have to myself."

He knew what she was hinting at, and gladly played right along. "I hope you're planning on spending those nights with me."

She went on tiptoe and kissed him, a little peck of a kiss. "I would not spend those nights with *anyone* but you."

A quick kiss was never enough. "Kiss me like you mean it."

She cast a glance around. "Well, I don't *think* anyone's looking."

"I don't give a damn if they are." He pulled her close and took the kiss he wanted—a long, slow, achingly sweet one.

Finally he had to take her by the waist and put her away from him. "I'd better go. I know you have to get to work."

She let out a rueful little sigh. "And you, too."

The conscience he wasn't supposed to have jabbed at him. "Right." He kissed the end of her nose, not daring to kiss anything else or he would scoop her up and carry her back to the guest house and keep her there all day long. "Tonight." He backed away, knowing he had to go, but jealous of losing sight of her.

"Tonight." She stood there in the shadow of the pines until he drove away.

That day went much like the day before. Sin returned to his hotel. He checked in with Rob. Then he went to that fitness club again to swim and lift weights.

A gray sedan pulled out into traffic behind him when he left the health club's parking lot. Sin drove slowly, signaling clearly at every turn, making it easy for whoever it was to trail right along. Glances in his rearview and side mirrors told him little. The driver was male, of medium build. He wore a tan shirt, had a crew cut. Dark glasses hid his eyes. He might have been twenty or forty or anywhere in between.

Finally, about two blocks from his hotel, Sin put on his blinker and carefully pulled to the shoulder of the road. The sedan drove on by. Sin looked over just as the car passed him. The eyes behind those dark glasses were looking right at him. Sin waved.

The gray car sped off.

Sin sat there for a moment before pulling out again. Whoever lurked behind those dark glasses understood now that Sin had spotted him.

And why in hell was he being followed in the first place? What was there to discover about his visit here—beyond the fact that he was having an affair with Ms. Sophie B. Jones?

Could that information be of use to someone in some way? Offhand, Sin didn't see how.

Sin had lunch at the hotel restaurant, then placed a call to his second in command at Inkerris, Incorporated. His associate said just what he expected him to say. The two projects they had in the works were running smoothly and he couldn't think of any reason someone might put a detective on Sin.

"But I'll be happy to check into it more thoroughly."

Sin told him not to bother. "If it becomes necessary, I'll handle it at this end."

When he hung up, he found himself wondering

about Sophie, remembering all the questions he saw in her eyes—questions he knew she was careful not to ask for fear she might chase him away.

Could she have decided to get some answers another way?

No. He couldn't believe that. Not Sophie. She didn't have a devious bone in her body.

Sin chose an orange from the fruit basket on the coffee table. Staring through a sliding glass door at the small garden patio outside his suite, he slowly began removing the peel.

He'd learned early that it didn't pay to trust anybody. People did what they had to do to get what they wanted. If you put your trust in them, they would only betray you, one way or another. He'd seen it time and time again. It was how the world worked.

Yet, in spite of his very real and practical cynicism, Sin trusted Sophie Jones. He could find no deceit when he looked in her eyes. Though it went against all he'd trained himself to believe, he simply could not picture her hiring somebody to follow him around.

Besides, he thought wryly as he separated off a slice of orange, Sophie couldn't *afford* to have him followed. She spent every cent she had trying to keep her precious Mountain Star in the black—and feeding every stray creature, human or otherwise, that wandered into her life.

No, whoever had decided to find out his business in Northern California, it wasn't Sophie B. Jones.

Sin ate his orange. He made a few more calls.

And then he waited.

Until he could see her again.

* * *

That night went by like the ones before it—too swiftly, even though Sin and Sophie had more time with that impossible theater of hers closed. They walked down to the spot by the creek and sat there for an hour. Then they wandered back to her little house, where they stayed until daylight.

In the morning, as the sun rose, they rode out, taking a different series of trails than the time before, though they did cross the pretty little pasture where so many roses grew wild. He left her around eight and returned to his hotel to pass the day somehow.

Until he could see her again.

The day seemed to drag on forever. He didn't see a single late-model gray sedan. His shadow had either given up—or become a lot more careful.

That night Sophie asked him if he had any family left at all.

"No. There's no one."

She was lying on her stomach, her chin propped on her hands. She rolled to the side and sat up, tugging on the sheet so it would cover those high, full breasts. "I used to be the same way."

Since he had most of his mind on that sheet—and the tempting prospect of peeling it back—it took Sin a few seconds to really hear her words. Then he frowned. *"Used to be?"*

"Yep." She wiggled around a little, pulling the damn sheet even higher.

"Sophie. That makes no sense. You either have a family or you don't."

"I don't." She was smiling way too smugly. "But I do."

He thought he took her meaning then. "I understand. Caleb's like a brother. And Myra thinks of you as a daughter.''

She wiggled around some more. The sheet slipped a little. She caught it, pulled it back up. "I do think of them as family—but I wasn't referring to them a minute ago.''

"Damn it, you're driving me crazy with that sheet.''

She went wide-eyed. "I am?"

"You know you are.''

Her lashes fluttered down. "I do?" She let the sheet fall. And she looked right at him.

He swore low with feeling. And then he reached for her.

Some time later, she lay beneath him, the sheet all tangled around their feet. She sighed and stroked his back. "What I meant was…''

He made a sleepy noise of complete contentment.

She poked him in the shoulder. "Sinclair. I'm trying to talk to you." She nudged him again. "Come on. Listen. Please.''

He let out a few grouchy groans, but then she whispered, so sweetly, "Please.''

He slid to the side and propped his head on his hand. "All right. What?"

She reached down for the sheet, found it and pulled it over them. "Remember, before you distracted me—"

"*I* distracted *you?*"

She giggled. "Well, all right. Before we distracted each other, I was talking about how I used to think I had no family, but I do, after all?''

"I remember." Though it made no sense at all. He

had paid well to learn all the facts about her. Those facts included parents long deceased and a beloved aunt who'd died when she was twenty-one—and that was it, as far as relatives went.

"Sophie, what are you driving at?"

"Well, I have an *honorary* family."

"This is getting more incomprehensible by the moment."

She smoothed the sheet, flipped her hair back over her shoulder. "If you'll just listen, I'll explain."

"I'm listening."

"Good. I suppose you never heard of the family they call the Jones Gang."

"Is this a joke?"

"No. I promise. This is for real."

"The Jones *Gang?*"

"Well, that's just what people call them. Most of them live in North Magdalene, up Highway Forty-Nine, between Nevada City and—"

"I've heard of North Magdalene."

"Well, okay. Did you know that there are a lot of Joneses there?"

"No, I have to admit I didn't know that."

"Well, there are. A *lot* of Joneses. And they've kind of adopted me. Because I'm a Jones, too, though I'm not a real blood relation."

He thought that over. "You've been adopted. By the *Jones Gang.*"

"Yes. That's exactly right. I have been adopted... informally, of course."

"Of course. Why the Jones Gang?"

"Why did they adopt me?"

"No, why are they called the Jones Gang?"

"Because they're a pretty wild bunch—or they were, until they all found love and settled down."

"Wild?"

"Yes. Bad actors. Hooligans. One step away from being outlaws. You know?"

"I suppose."

"I want to take you there."

"You do?" The idea of driving up Highway Forty-Nine to meet a family of hooligans didn't particularly excite him.

She must have seen his reluctance in his face, because she nudged him with her elbow. "Come with me. Tomorrow, in the afternoon. I think I can swing a few hours away from here, if I work like crazy all morning—how about you? Do you think you can manage to get away?"

From waiting all day until he could see her again? It shouldn't be too difficult.

"Please?"

He couldn't resist the appeal in those eyes. "I think I can find the time."

Her smile took his breath away. "I'm so glad—oh, and maybe we could swim. In the river." The Yuba River wound its way in and out of the canyons along the highway. "It's the best time of year for it."

"I'll bring something to swim in."

"Oh, I just know you're going to love the Joneses."

"We'll see."

"Sinclair. You're so cautious."

"Sophie. You love everybody."

"Maybe so. But the Jones family is special. Just you wait and see."

* * *

At two the next afternoon, they walked into a bar called the Hole in the Wall, which stood in the middle of Main Street in the tiny mountain town of North Magdalene.

Sophie had already explained to Sin that the bar—and the restaurant next door—were Jones-owned businesses. As were the gift shop across the street, the service station a few doors down, the one motel and the gold sales store up near the end of town—which was easily visible from the beginning of town, as North Magdalene wasn't much more than a bend in the road. The sign at the foot of Main Street read, Welcome To North Magdalene, Population 229. Smokey Says Fire Danger Is High.

Inside the Hole in the Wall, Sophie bounced right up to the bar, towing Sin along behind her. "Hello, Jared," she said to the tall, rangy character with the steel gray eyes who stood behind the beer taps.

Those steely eyes softened. "Sophie B. Jones. How've you been?"

"Just terrific. This is Sinclair. Sinclair Riker." The bartender nodded and Sin nodded back. "Where's Oggie?" All during the short drive up there, she had babbled away about the wonderful Oggie Jones, patriarch of the Jones Gang, the sweetest, wisest, most delightfully eccentric old man in the whole world.

Jared twitched a thumb in the direction of a green curtain strung along the back wall. "The old man's playing poker. Not to be disturbed—for a while, anyway. Why don't you two grab a couple of stools and have a beer on the house?"

Sophie considered, then shook her head. "Thanks, but I think I'll show Sinclair around town now and then take him swimming. We'll come back later." Just then a tall, pretty woman with strawberry blond hair emerged through the door behind the bar. "Eden!" Sophie smiled wide in greeting.

"Hello, Sophie B. It's good to see you."

Sophie made the introductions. Eden was Jared's wife and helped him run the bar and the restaurant next door. She shook hands with Sin, and then asked, "So, can you two hang around for dinner?"

Sophie looked at Sin. He gave her a fine-with-me shrug.

"Around seven? We'll throw some steaks on the grill and open a bottle of wine."

"We'd love it."

"I'll invite the old man, too," Jared said. "As soon as he gets through cheating at poker."

"That would be terrific."

"Do you remember how to get to our place?"

Sophie said she did, then she grabbed Sin's hand again and dragged him out into the sunlight.

They trooped up and down Main Street. They went in Fletcher Gold Sales, where Sophie introduced him to Sam Fletcher, who was married to the remarkable Oggie's only daughter, Delilah. They stopped at Wishbook, the gift and sundries shop, which was run by Evie Jones Riggins, Oggie's niece. They even peeked in at the counter of the garage and exchanged greetings with Patrick Jones, Oggie's third son—the others being Jack Roper, the sheriff's deputy, who was illegitimate, but still very much a part of the family, Jared, the bartender, and Brendan, who drove a big rig for a living. Each of them was married, and most of them had children.

Sophie rattled off names and relationships as if she'd known every one of them for her whole life. Sin smiled and shook people's hands and tried to keep the names straight. He also wondered why the hell he was enjoying himself so much, wandering around this tiny town, meeting strangers he was never likely to see again.

But then all he had to do was glance at the woman beside him and it all came clear. Her pleasure was infectious. She adored these people and he couldn't help liking them, too.

They used the rest rooms at the garage to change into their swimsuits. Then they got back in his rental car. She directed him down a street called Bullfinch Lane, across a bridge to the other side of the river.

"This is Sweetbriar Park. Just pull in there."

He parked the car and then she led him along a path that finally opened up to a sandy beach at the river's edge. There, in the shade of the oaks that grew near the sand, two women sat in fold-up lawn chairs. Out in the bright sunlight, a number of children of varying ages made castles of sand and splashed in the shallows. Across the gleaming water, several older kids sunned themselves on the rocks.

Sin felt a sharp stab of disappointment. He'd imagined they might actually manage a little time alone.

No such luck. Right away, one of the women looked their way and waved. "Sophie B.! Hello!"

Sophie dragged him over and introduced him to Regina Jones, Patrick's wife, and also to Amy Jones, who was married to Brendan, the truck driver. The older kids on the other side of the river dived in and swam across, to be introduced as well.

Finally, after he'd met Regina's stepdaughters and their teenage girlfriends, admired several life-jacketed toddlers and said hello to two boys named Pete and Mark, who were also related to Joneses in some way he didn't quite catch, he was allowed to spread his towel in the warm sand.

Sophie yanked off the big beach shirt she'd worn over her cute blue suit and tossed it to the ground. "Last one in's a claim jumper!" She raced for the water's edge and dived in so quickly, he'd lost the game before he even realized he was playing it.

He took off and hit the water fast. Damn, he'd forgotten how cold the Yuba could be! She was halfway to the big rocks on the opposite bank, swimming in strong, even strokes across the current, before he caught up with her. He seized her ankle and gave it a tug.

She went under. Five seconds later, she came up sputtering. "No fair!" She tried to splash him.

He caught her arm and reeled her in closer—though not as close as he'd have liked to. After all, there were those two Jones women and all those little Joneses sitting back there in the sand.

"Sinclair!" She faked outrage, wriggling and squirming—and laughing in spite of herself.

He'd lost hold of her ankle, but he kept a firm grip on her arm. "So I'm a claim jumper, am I?"

She batted her water-soaked eyelashes. "If the shoe fits—"

"You cheated."

"No, you just weren't fast enough."

"You have to say 'go,' or it doesn't count."

She stuck out her tongue at him as the current tugged at them, trying to pull them along.

"That does it." He put his other hand on her head and pushed. She went under—and reached out and pulled him down along with her. They wrestled in the cold water, air bubbles bouncing all around them, her long hair snaking and swirling, caressing his shoulder, floating against his cheek.

Finally they both shot to the surface, gulping in air—and laughing. His hand held her waist, hers was pressed against his heart.

"Oh, Sinclair..." Her eyes went tender.

Like a bright light popping on in a dark room, the knowledge came to him: he was happy. Happy. Splashing in the icy water of the Yuba with Sophie, acting like a silly kid, while all those Joneses watched from the bank.

He moved forward, treading water, holding them both in place though the current kept trying to carry them down. "Sophie." Their lips met, cold and wet on the surface, so warm underneath. He pulled back.

She said, "I can't help it. I *have* to say it—I love you, Sinclair."

He kept treading water, thinking of all the lies he'd told, of the kind of man she thought he was and the man he really was. Of how this could never last. The truth would find them soon.

"Sophie, I—"

And then Regina Jones started screaming.

"Anthea, my God! Anthea!"

Sin turned just in time to see the orange life jacket and the small dark head of one of the toddlers, bouncing along toward the rapids a hundred yards downstream.

Chapter Eight

Sin and Sophie struck out as one, swimming fast down the center of the stream. Sin was vaguely aware of the others on the bank, but they didn't have the chance he and Sophie did, with the strong power of the current beneath them, pushing them along. The others in the shallows would have to swim out to get the river's aid.

Within twenty feet, they left the depths behind. The river flattened out and the streambed came up to meet them. They ran with their feet and swam with their hands until the water level dropped so low there was nothing they could do but stumble along, falling on the slippery rocks beneath their feet, gaining an unstable purchase and then surging forward once more.

Ahead of them, the life jacket bobbed, the little head going facedown, popping upright again, then floating back, so the tiny nose pointed at the blue sky above. Sin could hear the crying now—and the choking each time the small head went down and came up again.

Sin shoved at the rocks with his legs, pushing himself onward, leaving Sophie behind.

Luck shined on him in the form of two boulders sticking out above the surface with several dead branches wedged between them. The orange life jacket got stuck in the eddy created by the rocks and the debris. For several blessed seconds, the child swirled in a circle, the life jacket almost catching on a tree branch, the child sputtering and choking, gone past crying now.

But it couldn't last. Too soon, the relentless current had its way. The little body spun on out of the eddy and went tumbling downstream once more.

By then, though, Sin had come within a few feet. He shoved again with his legs, lunging forward. By some miracle, he caught a strap that trailed off the back of the life jacket. He gave a yank and then he had the child around the waist.

He got the little body onto his shoulder just as he lost his footing—his legs went straight out in front of him and he rolled along on his rear end for several more yards, his feet scrambling for purchase again as he struggled to keep his burden above the water.

And then he felt Sophie's hand, grabbing his swim trunks from behind. He stopped rushing downstream and immediately wedged his feet in behind a couple of rocks to hold him there. He looked back. She had herself braced firmly against the rocks, as well.

"Give me Anthea," she instructed. "You're stronger than me. You can pull us all back to the bank."

He handed the child over. Sophie hoisted her to one shoulder and then held out her hand. They didn't get three steps before the others met them in the middle of the stream with the water rushing fast all around. They made a chain and passed the little girl, who'd started choking and coughing again, back to the safety of her mother's arms.

On the beach, one of Regina's stepdaughters—the younger one, Marnie—was crying. "I turned around. It was just for a minute. And then she was gone. Oh, Anthy…" She spoke to the toddler, who sat on her mother's shoulder by then, looking soggy but otherwise all right, sucking furiously on her thumb. "Anthy, I'm so sorry…."

In answer, Anthea pulled her thumb from her mouth and offered it to Marnie.

"No, thanks," Marnie said, smiling through her tears—and then she was reaching out for her stepmother, "Gina, I know I said I'd watch her. It's all my fault. I'm so sorry…."

Somehow Regina managed to embrace her stepdaughter with one arm while she held the smaller child cradled in the other. "It's all right," Regina soothed the older girl. "She's safe. She's all right." She looked up, caught Sin's eye. "Thanks to you."

A grateful chorus of agreement went up, from all those other Joneses. Sophie still held his hand. She gave it a squeeze. He glanced into her shining eyes— and for one, brief, impossible moment, he saw the man she thought he was reflected there.

That night, Regina and Patrick and their daughters joined them for steaks at Jared and Eden's house. The story of Anthea's rescue was recounted more than once—by Marnie first, and then by Regina when old Oggie Jones arrived and demanded to hear it, too.

Later, after dinner, feeling a little uncomfortable with all the praise and gratitude the Joneses kept showering on him, Sin wandered outside alone. He found a place at the railing of Jared's deck and stood staring out at the pines, thinking that soon he'd go in and find Sophie so they could be on their way.

"I guess you showed up in town just when we needed you." The rough voice of Oggie Jones came from beside him. Odd. The old man walked with a cane that announced his appearance wherever he went—yet Sin hadn't heard him approach.

Sin turned his head and met the old man's strange small eyes. "It was mostly luck."

"Luck don't mean squat if a man doesn't act fast." Those too-wise eyes seemed to bore right down into him. "You acted fast. And this family thanks you for it."

"Anyone else would have done the same thing."

"But *could* anyone else have done the same thing?"

What was that supposed to mean? Sin didn't think he needed to know. "It worked out all right." He felt ready and willing to drop the subject for good. "That's what matters."

The old man let out a low, amused cackle of a laugh. "Good point. And how about for you?"

"What?"

"How's it working out for you?"

Sin faced him squarely. "Are you getting at something here?"

"What do you think, Mr. *Sin*clair Riker?"

Sin noted the emphasis on the first half of his name

and felt the skin along his shoulder blades tighten. No one here knew him as Sin.

He recalled that gray sedan. Someone had decided to have him followed. Could this strange character who thought of himself as Sophie's uncle be that someone? Coldly he suggested, "I think if there's something you want to say to me, you had better say it outright."

The old man pondered that suggestion, then grunted. "Son, you don't know me at all." He pulled a cigar from his shirt pocket and began peeling the cellophane wrapper off. Sin watched those gnarled hands rumple the wrapper and tuck it away in another pocket. "Sophie B. tells me that you are the Sinclair Riker whose family once owned the ranch where she lives now."

"That's right."

Oggie bit the end off the cigar and spat it over his shoulder, beyond the deck. "And how long you stayin' in our beautiful county?"

"I'm not sure."

"Where *you* livin' now, anyway?"

"Los Angeles."

"And you're here to buy property, Sophie B. says. Is that so?"

"Possibly."

The old man cackled some more. Out in the trees, an owl hooted. Sin looked toward the sound—and away from whatever those wise eyes thought they knew. He heard the hiss of a match striking, saw the quick flare of light in his side vision. And then the smell of smoke wafted his way.

The rough voice spoke again. "When a man falls

in love, it changes everything. Changes *him*. You know what I mean?''

Sin faced Sophie's ''uncle'' once more, but said nothing. Wherever the old man was headed with this gambit, Sin felt certain he could get there all on his own.

Oggie studied the burning end of his cigar. ''Let me tell you a little story.''

''If I said no, would it matter?''

''Hell, no.'' He flicked his ash. ''You listenin'?''

Sin shrugged.

''I'll take that as a yes.'' Oggie leaned against the railing, sucked in smoke and blew it out. ''I come here, to North Magdalene, when I was thirty-five, a footloose gamblin' man. I saw my wife-to-be the first day I walked into town. I knew she would be mine the minute I laid eyes on her. What I didn't realize until later was that I would be hers as well.

''Beautiful Bathsheba...'' Oggie gestured grandly. The red end of the cigar made bright trails through the darkness. ''...the empress of my heart.'' He shook his head. ''She's been gone for nigh on thirty years now. But in here—'' he tapped his chest with the heel of his hand— ''In here, she lives on. Because of her, I am the man you see before you now. Because of her, I put down roots. And those roots go deep, deep as if I had been born in these parts. Because of her, I got...commitments.'' He said the word with reverence. Then he turned from the night to look at Sin again. ''And because of her, I just might go on forever—meddlin' where people wish to hell I'd get lost.'' He let out another of those low cackles, and leaned in closer to Sin. ''That is what you're thinkin', ain't it? That you wish to hell I'd mind my own business.''

Sin couldn't help smiling. ''You don't strike me as a man likely to be affected by what other people think.''

The old man thought that was funny. He cackled again, louder this time.

Sin added, ''And love may have changed you. But I am not you.''

The old man thought that was *really* funny. He threw back his head and brayed at the moon.

Watching him, Sin felt the tension that had coiled inside him fade away to nothing at all. Oggie Jones was just a sentimental old character who liked to hear himself talk. He knew no more about Sin than anyone else did. And the odds were very small that he'd hired some P.I. to follow Sin around.

And even if he had, what could he have found out? The name of Sin's hotel, the health club he visited— and that he'd been spending his nights in the slim, soft arms of Sophie B. Jones.

The hotel and the health club meant nothing. And anyone who saw him with Sophie could have figured out the rest.

The old man puffed on his cigar a while longer. The smoke trailed toward the moon. At last, he said, ''It's after ten. I'll bet you want to get goin'.''

''Yes. We should probably be on our way.''

''Well, come on, then. Let's go inside and find that woman of yours.''

''Did you like my adopted family?'' Sophie asked as they drove the twisting road back to the Mountain Star.

"Yes," he said honestly. "I liked them."

"I'm glad." She leaned across the console and rested her head on his shoulder. "What did you think of Oggie?"

He recalled those wise eyes, that cackling laugh. "He's one of a kind."

She lifted her head, brushed a hand against his shoulder. "I just love him."

"I gathered."

She sighed. "I know he rubs some people the wrong way. But I think he really *cares*. I think he would do anything for the people he loves."

Sin felt for her hand, brought it to his lips, then had to let go to negotiate the next sharp turn. "I think you're right."

"You do?"

He nodded, keeping his eyes front to watch the road. She settled her head on his shoulder again.

They drove the rest of the way in silence.

By the time he pulled into the drive that led up to the Mountain Star, she had dropped off to sleep. She didn't stir as he parked the car, or when he turned the key and the engine went quiet.

"Sophie..." he whispered.

She moved a little, made a small, sleepy sound of protest, then snuggled against his shoulder as if it were her pillow for the night.

"Sophie, we're here."

She said something unintelligible, and finally lifted her head. "I went to sleep."

"No kidding."

She yawned and stretched.

He said, "You're still half-asleep."

She gave him a look that had nothing to do with sleeping. "Let's go to bed."

Once they got inside, she wanted a shower. They took one together. He lathered her hair twice for her, the sweet-smelling bubbles running down his arms. Then, when they stepped out onto the bathroom tiles, they dried each other.

Soon enough they were kissing, and laughing, the towels dropping at their feet.

He carried her to the bedroom and laid her on the bed. She looked up at him, lifting her arms, her still-wet hair snaking on the pillow, reminding him...

Of the two of them, wrestling underwater, the bubbles rising all around them, her hair floating against his chest.

Happy.

He was happy.

Living a lie with Sophie B. Jones.

"Sinclair..." she beckoned him.

He sank down upon her, burying his face in the wet, coiling strands of her hair. She pulled him close, sighing.

And when her fulfillment shuddered through her, she said it again.

"I love you, love you, love you, I do...."

In the morning, they went riding. And he stayed for breakfast after.

She kissed him goodbye before he left, in the grove of pines near his car, her sweet body pressing close, her hair smelling of sunshine and last night's shampoo.

"It's a new movie tonight," she told him, pulling back just enough that she could look up at him.

"I know, I saw the ad in the *Union*. The next installment in—"

"Our Randi Wilding Film Retrospective." She looked exceedingly pleased with herself. "Tonight, it's *Kerrigan's Honor*. Randi plays an FBI agent whose mother and sister are raped and murdered by a gang of thugs. Naturally, she has to kill them all…in very imaginative ways."

"Naturally."

"You're going to love this one, I just know it. And next week, we'll have—"

"Stop. Let's take it one week at a time."

Something happened in her eyes then. Their brightness dimmed a little. She looked down at where her hands rested against his chest, and then back up at him. "Sinclair?"

"What?"

And she dared to ask, "Is there going to *be* a next week for us?"

What could he say to that? How the hell did he know?

She fiddled with a button on his shirt. "I don't want to push you. I honestly don't, but…" And it all came pouring out. "Oh, Sinclair, I have to tell you, sometimes, when you leave, all I can think is how much I *don't* know about you. I don't even know where you live—well, LA, I know that. But LA is so big. What part of LA? And what is your house like? Do you know your neighbors? Are they nice? And where do you work? What do you really *do* there? And your friends. What are your friends like? Will I ever meet them? Will they hate me or like me?"

"Sophie. No one could hate you."

"Sinclair, do you understand what I'm asking you?"

He knew then that he could put off telling her no longer.

But where to begin?

"Sinclair, can you understand?"

"Yes. Of course, I can."

"Could we talk? Really talk? About the two of us. About...what will happen next? Could we talk...tonight?"

"Sophie..."

She put up a hand between them, for silence. "Tonight. All right?"

He thought of the long day of work she had ahead of her. At least, if he waited till tonight, she'd have a few hours to herself after everything had been said. Maybe that was the best way. If there was such a thing in this situation.

Or maybe he was just putting off the inevitable again....

"Please, Sinclair."

"All right, Sophie. Tonight."

"Thank you." She moved close again to brush a kiss against his lips. It wasn't enough for him—when it came to her, nothing was ever enough. He grabbed her close and kissed her hard.

Then, as she had other mornings, she stood beneath the pines to watch him go.

Sin drove back to his hotel by rote, hardly seeing where he was going, thinking of the obsession that had got hold of him the day he'd learned his family's ranch could be his again. The timing had seemed perfect. He had the money and the time to build himself a big new house, fill the stables with thoroughbred horses and live the life of the gentleman rancher. His second in command at Inkerris, Incorporated, would be taking over from him. Within a year he'd hardly have to travel to LA at all. Within a year, no matter what kind of fight she had tried to put up, he would have been able to remove the one obstacle to his plans: Ms. Sophie B. Jones and her five-acre lease.

He'd intended only to get rid of her.

But now he couldn't bear to lose her.

Love changes a man, old Oggie Jones had said.

But Sin was a realist. No one changed that much in five days. He still wanted his land back, wanted his *heritage* back.

And love? It was a word people batted around a lot. His father had talked about love all the time—the love of family, the love of the land. And then he'd lost the land and opted out by hanging himself. And his mother had *loved;* she'd loved him and his father—and she'd claimed to love the first ten or so of the string of men who'd put food on her table.

By the time he was nine years old, Sin had learned that love was something it didn't pay to believe in, something he simply did not have time for if he planned to crawl out of the hole his father and mother had put him in. He got his first paper route when he was ten, and he was working as a busboy by the time he was sixteen.

He'd been careful to stay on the right side of the law. He'd given a wide berth to the drug dealers in his neighborhood—and not out of any nobility of spirit. There was fast money in drugs, and money of any kind interested him. But unfortunately drug money was fast money he could lose if he got caught. And he couldn't afford a prison record following him around. After all, he wanted to rebuild for himself the fortune his father had lost. So he kept his nose clean.

He bought his first house, a run-down rental duplex in San Pedro when he was twenty-one. He forced the tenants out over their constant—and sincere—protests that they had nowhere to go. Then he fixed the place up himself, reselling it a year after he bought it for three times what he'd paid for it.

By eight years ago, when he was thirty, Inkerris, Incorporated, was going strong. He'd come a long way. In the next eight years, he went even farther. And *love* had played no part at all in his success.

No, Sin Riker didn't believe in love and he didn't have time for it. And he certainly didn't deserve it— a fact that Sophie was going to have to face tonight when he told her the truth.

Three times, she had told him she loved him. After tonight, he doubted she'd be telling him again.

Sin parked his car in the hotel's lot and went in the main entrance, where he stopped at the front desk.

"Sinclair Riker, room 103," he told the clerk. "Any messages?"

The clerk pointed toward the small sitting area opposite the desk. "Someone to see you."

Sin turned just as his former fiancée stood from a damask-covered wing chair. "Sin, darling. Where *have* you been? I've been waiting for over an hour."

Chapter Nine

"Willa. I had no idea you were coming."

"Oh, I'm sure you didn't." After pausing to brush lightly at the few wrinkles that had dared to crease the front of her pencil-thin silk skirt, Willa strolled up to him and slid a proprietary arm through his. "We have to talk." She scrunched up her perfect nose. "What's that I smell? Horse, I do believe."

He looked down into her exotically slanted blue eyes. "I've been riding."

"*Riding?*" She squeezed his arm, raised a black eyebrow. "Oh, I have no doubt at all about that."

The light dawned. "You hired a detective service to have me followed."

"I certainly did." She made a tsking sound with her tongue. "And it cost me a serious chunk of change, too. I was assured you'd never know. But then you spotted him anyway—on Monday, wasn't it?''

"Sunday, actually. Monday was the day I let him know that I knew."

She ran a long, red, beautifully manicured fingernail down his arm. "I should probably demand at least half of my money back."

"What do you want, Willa?"

She lifted a shoulder in a delicate shrug. "I told you. We have to talk."

"All right." He started to move toward the sitting area just a few feet away.

She hung back, casting a glance at the desk clerk. "Privately, please—how about your room?"

He dragged in a long breath and let it out slowly. "Fine. Let's go."

In his suite, Willa tossed her envelope bag on an end table, kicked off her Italian pumps and dropped to the sofa, stretching her long, silk-clad legs out along its length. Once she'd made herself comfortable, she got right to the point. "You've been having an affair, Sin. With that sweet little nobody who's living at that ranch of yours."

Sin leaned against the closed door and folded his arms over his chest. "*Sweet*, Willa? Was that how your detective described her?"

"I have pictures."

He shook his head in disgust. "God, Willa."

Willa recrossed her legs, ran a smoothing hand up her already smooth stockings, then looked up to make sure he saw the provocative gesture. "She's not your type at all. So *nice*. Big innocent eyes. Acres of long badly cut hair. And those outré calf-length dresses that look as if they were made from Laura Ashley window treatments. Honestly, Sin. I'm disappointed in you."

Sin straightened from the door. "Is that all you got me up here to tell me?"

Willa sighed and cast a glance heavenward. "Isn't it enough?"

"You're completely off base here, and you know it. How I spend my time—and who I spend it with—are no longer any of your concern."

She swung her legs to the floor and rose, catlike, to her feet. "Of course what you do is my concern. I'm your fiancée."

"What the hell are you talking about?"

"Sin, please. Let's not play games. You know I'm going to marry you."

"I am not the one who's playing games."

"Oh, Sin." She dipped her chin and looked up at him archly from under her lashes. "You know I only play the games you like." She sauntered toward him.

"Stop."

She paused, put a hand on her hip and pretended to look confused. "What, darling?"

"Let me refresh your memory."

"My memory is fresh enough."

"*You* called it off, Willa. You said, and I quote, 'I have no intention of moving to the middle of nowhere to raise horses in the pine trees. If that's what you think you want, then you and I are through.'"

Willa sighed. "I was just trying to get you to come to your senses."

"You failed."

"I can see that. And I'm willing to…reevaluate my position on this issue."

"It's too late."

She shook her smooth cap of black hair. "No, it's not." And then, in a stunningly swift move, she reached behind her. He heard the zipper of that clinging silk dress as it started to slide.

"No, Willa."

"Yes, Sin."

The zipper parted all the way. The dress slid off her shoulders. She pushed it down, over her boyish hips and her perfect legs. Within seconds, she stepped free of it. Now she wore only a black garter belt and silk stockings. Her small, perfect breasts pointed right at him.

She was a beautiful woman. And she left him absolutely cold. He wondered abstractly what he'd ever seen in her. "Put your dress back on, Willa."

"After I'm done here."

"You are done. Believe me."

She started toward him again.

"Willa. Don't do this."

She didn't stop until she was against him, her impudent breasts pressed into his shirtfront, her grasping hand finding him through the fabric of his slacks.

Flaccid. She felt that. And the confident gleam in her eyes faded a little.

"It's no good, Willa." He had a powerful urge to shove her away, but he controlled it. She expected the old games to work on him. He couldn't really blame her for that. They'd always worked before.

Her hand moved, stroking, squeezing, trying to inspire some response. But there was none. At last, she let go and stepped back. "Your little *sweetheart* must be very…demanding."

"Leave Sophie out of this." He kept his tone gentle, but she couldn't have mistaken the underlying thread of steel in it. "And put your dress back on."

A tight, feral sound escaped her red mouth. Sin thought for a moment she might make some remark about Sophie that he wouldn't be able to let pass. But no words came. Finally she turned and stalked back to where she'd left her dress. She bent down, shook it out and stepped into it. She reached behind her. He heard the zipper close. Then she ran her hands down her waist and hips, straightening, smoothing.

She went to the sofa, collected her shoes, slid them on and grabbed up her bag. It was only a few steps to the door. She stopped with her hand on the knob to grant him one final caustic glare.

"You will regret this," she said.

All he felt was sadness, for both of them. Two hard, acquisitive people. They'd struck sparks off each other once, sparks that had ignited to a white-hot blaze. But there had been no warmth to it. Only heat without comfort, like the heartless fires of hell.

"Do you hear me, Sin Riker? You will be sorry."

"Willa, I swear to you, I already am."

"Not sorry enough, I'm afraid." She went out the door, slamming it smartly behind her.

She'd been gone a good ten minutes before Sin admitted to himself how very simple it would be for Willa to make him sorrier still.

About an hour after Sinclair had left for the day, Sophie sat on a stool in the hayloft, checking the sprockets on her aging projector, trying to figure out which one might be sticking. Last Sunday, the old monster had nearly burned a hole in the first reel.

Naturally though, right now, it seemed to be working all right.

"Hello? Is anyone up there?" It was a woman's voice, one Sophie didn't recognize. The voice came from the foot of the ladder that led up to the loft.

Sophie rose from the stool and went to the top of the ladder. A tall, black-haired fashion plate of a woman stood below. "Sophie B. Jones?"

"That's me."

"The big man at the stables said I might find you here. I wonder, could I steal a few minutes of your time?"

"Sure. Be right down." Sophie returned to the projector, swiftly rewound the short bit of test reel and turned the thing off.

The woman watched from the foot of the ladder as Sophie climbed down. "You actually run a movie theater in here?"

Sophie jumped from the last rung, brushed off her hands and shook out her long skirt. "You bet."

The woman looked up toward the rafters and then right at Sophie. "Charming." Her inflection said she found the barn—and Sophie herself—anything but.

Sophie moved back a step. "You didn't say your name."

"Willa. Willa Tweed."

The name rang a bell somewhere far back in her mind, but Sophie couldn't quite remember why. She gestured at the rows of theater seats that marched away from them, down toward the screen. "Have a chair."

Willa Tweed licked her lips—nervously, it seemed to Sophie. "No. I think it's better if I stand." She took in a long breath and let it out slowly. "I have to admit, now that I'm here, I simply do not know how to begin...." She let the words trail off. A long, significant pause ensued, a pause in which Sophie's own uneasiness increased. Finally the woman spoke again. "I've come about Sin."

Sophie felt more confused by the moment. Was the woman a representative of some religious group? "About sin? I'm afraid I don't—"

"Sin," Willa Tweed said again, impatiently. "Sin Riker."

"You mean...Sinclair?"

The woman's mouth tightened. "Yes. Sinclair Riker. My fiancé. That's exactly who I mean."

Right then, Sophie remembered where she'd heard the woman's name before:

"There was someone," Sinclair had said. *"It didn't work out."*

And Sophie had asked, *"What was her name?"*

He had answered, *"Willa."*

Sophie said very carefully, "I don't understand. Sinclair told me it was over between you and him."

The woman laughed, a brittle angry sound. "Oh, I'm sure he did. I'm sure he told you whatever he thought you wanted to hear."

Sophie fell back a step. "No. I don't believe that. I don't believe he would—"

Willa threw up a hand. "You have no idea what Sin is capable of." She made a low, derisive sound. "Honestly. Your own situation says it all."

Sophie's heart was pounding way too fast. She put a hand against it, in a pointless effort to make it slow down. "My own situation?"

"The problem that Sin came here to handle in the first place—you."

"Me?" Sophie shook her head. "He came here to handle *me*?"

"Yes. You and your inconvenient five-acre lease on his precious ranch. Of course, he would have offered you a good price for it. Did you take it? If you haven't, I suppose he must think you will. I suppose right now he thinks he can talk you into just about anything. And I also imagine he's right...don't you?"

Sophie tried to comprehend what the woman was babbling about. "No. It's not his ranch. Not anymore. Not for years and years. You don't understand, he—"

The woman laughed again. "*I'm* not the one who doesn't understand. Sin owns this ranch now. And if you don't know that, you're a bigger fool than I ever imagined. My God, you must be making lease payments—to Inkerris, Incorporated. Don't you get it? It's an anagram. For his name."

"His name," Sophie echoed numbly.

"Exactly. Sin Riker. Inkerris. Switch the letters around a little and you can have either one."

Sophie felt weak in the knees. A rickety folding chair stood not far away. She backed up quickly and dropped into it.

Willa Tweed watched her through glittering ice blue eyes. "So, I can see that the anagram got past you. And it appears that Sin has told you virtually nothing."

"I don't—"

"Let me fully enlighten you."

"No, I—"

The woman ignored Sophie's weak protest and continued right on. "About six months ago, Sin saw some notice—in the *San Francisco Chronicle*, I believe it was, though I can't be sure. He takes a lot of newspapers. He finds potential properties in them."

Right then Tom, the black cat, poked his head through the split in the curtains that led to the outside doors. He let out a small, curious *"Mnneow?"*

Willa glanced back briefly, saw it was only a cat, and then turned on Sophie once more. "But I'm getting off the point, which is that Sin found a for sale notice about the *former* Riker Ranch in that paper. And from then on, he was a man obsessed. He wanted that land back."

Sophie's mind seemed to be working way too slowly. She asked idiotically, "He...wanted it back?"

The woman let out a delicate little grunt. "That's what I said. He wanted it back. So he got his people on it."

"His people?"

"Oh, come on. You understand. He has people who work for him, people whose job it is to investigate any property that catches his interest. In the case of this ranch, his people found that the only problem was you. Somehow you had managed to get yourself a lease on five acres of this place. Sin didn't like that at all. He wanted to know more about you—about how you were going to take it when he told you he wanted to terminate that lease. So he investigated further. He had a detective service following you around for six weeks."

The idea made Sophie's stomach roil: someone, some total stranger, had watched her go about her life for a month and a half. How could that have been? "No..."

"Yes. He learned that you were very...attached to

the little enterprise you've created here. And that it would probably be difficult to get rid of you until your lease was up. Which would be another ten years. But Sin didn't care. He bought the property anyway, a very low-key acquisition through intermediaries. He used a San Francisco bank to handle the whole transaction so that, until he was ready to approach you with his offer, you'd know next to nothing about the new owner.''

Tom strolled up to Willa and began rubbing at her ankles. She delicately kicked him away. The cat moved on to Sophie, jumping onto her lap. Sophie absently stroked his warm fur. The purring started, a warm, friendly sound—in direct contrast to the frosty blue of Willa Tweed's eyes.

Willa went on. "Sin finds that works quite well—to come in with the deed in his hand and all the leverage he can muster lined up behind him. Then he makes his offer. And the smart ones take what he offers.''

Sophie held Tom tighter. The cat purred louder.

Willa asked, "Shall I tell you what happens if they *don't* take his offer?''

Right then, the curtain to the concession area stirred again. Sinclair stepped through it.

Sophie's hold on Tom loosened. The cat slipped lightly to the floor and sauntered off toward the rows of seats. Sophie watched him go. So much easier to watch the cat than to look at Willa Tweed—or to meet the dark burning eyes of the man by the curtain.

Willa must have turned and seen Sinclair. Sophie heard her hard laugh. "Sin, darling. Come join us. I was just explaining the facts of life to your sweet little girlfriend here.''

When Sinclair didn't reply, Willa laughed again. "Well, it may be the middle of August, but I do believe I detect a certain chill in the air."

Tom disappeared down a row of seats. Sophie made herself look at Willa again. The dark-haired woman faced away, toward the man by the curtains to the concession stand. Her back was very straight and proud.

"I suppose it's time I was leaving," Willa said.

Sinclair moved clear of the curtains as Willa started his way. Just before she went through, she turned once more to Sinclair. "I do believe you're sorry enough—now."

Sinclair said flatly, "Goodbye, Willa."

"Yes," Willa replied. "I would say that's exactly the word for it." She pushed the curtain aside and stepped through.

Chapter Ten

Once Willa was gone, Sophie stayed in her chair, not moving, for a very long time. And Sinclair just stood there, near the last row of seats, as silent as she was.

Finally she made herself look at him, made herself ask in a voice that came out all weak and whispery, "Are you engaged to her?"

He met her gaze, unwavering. "I was."

"Until when?"

"She broke it off a couple of weeks ago."

"She said otherwise. She said you were still her fiancé."

"Then she lied."

Hope kindled in Sophie then, a hot, hungry little flame. Maybe it was *all* a lie, all those awful things the woman had said....

But, no. How could Willa have known the name

of the faceless corporation that owned the ranch now—unless Inkerris and Sin Riker were one and the same? Beyond that, there were all the details of his life that he hadn't told her. And most damning of all was Sinclair himself, standing there, looking so bleak, his expression telling Sophie better than words ever could that at least some of what Willa had said was true.

Sophie straightened in the chair, ordered some volume into her voice. "She also said that *you* are Inkerris, Incorporated. That you own the Riker Ranch now, that you came here with the intention of manipulating me into giving up my lease."

Tom appeared again, sidling up to Sinclair. Sinclair bent and lifted him into those strong arms. The cat immediately started purring. Sophie could hear it clearly from all the way over in her chair.

"Is it true, Sinclair? Is that really why you came here?"

He let the cat down. "Yes."

The single word pierced her like a blade to the heart. "Oh, Sin..." She heard herself call him by that name for the first time. And realized that it fit him. "Five days. Five whole days. We've been together every moment we could. You never told me. You never said a word."

She waited for him to explain. For him to simply say that he didn't tell her of his schemes because he couldn't figure out how to do it without running the risk of losing her.

Which was nothing but the truth.

However, the truth, at that point, wasn't good enough for Sin.

He stood at the top of the aisle in Sophie's barn

theater, looking into her wide, wounded eyes and he knew that the time for explanations had passed. At that moment, Sin Riker hated being inside his own skin.

"Please," she said in a broken voice. "Tell me. Explain to me why you—"

He put up a hand. "Sophie, it's no good."

"What?" Those innocent eyes pleaded with his. "No good? What's no good?"

"You know."

"No. I...I want to understand. I want you to tell me—"

"There's nothing to tell. Nothing that will make any difference. We're...night and day, you and me. And everything we had was based on lies. *My* lies."

"No. Don't say that. In your heart, you—"

"Sophie. Face it. It's just no good. Look at you. You pass out bag lunches to the homeless."

"So?"

"Sophie, I have never given anything away in my life."

"But...you had to fight, I understand that. You had nothing. And you had to make a place for yourself in the world."

He shook his head. "Look at you. Sitting there defending me. I don't deserve defending, Sophie."

She raised her chin, did her best to look defiant. "I believe you do."

"You *want* to believe. But believing won't change the facts. Maybe it's time you heard the truth. Maybe it's time I made it clear what I had in mind for you."

He could see the denial in her eyes, he could read her so well by then. Not if it's ugly, she was thinking. Not if it's cruel.

He goaded her. "Are you ready for the truth, Sophie?"

She pressed her lips together, looked away. Then she drew in a breath and faced him once more. "Yes. All right. Tell me the truth."

And he did, in a voice without expression. "The truth is, I was going to destroy you if I had to." He began walking toward her. "If you had refused my offer, you were going to find yourself in a world of woe trying to run this place."

She watched him advance, shaking her head. "No, you couldn't have. You *wouldn't* have."

He kept coming until he stood right in front of her, looking down. "Oh, yes, I would. I've done it before. And I've done it often."

She swallowed, eyes wide as saucers now, staring up at him as if he frightened her. "Driven people out, you mean?"

He nodded. "I've become quite…skilled at it, over the years."

Her sweet mouth was trembling. "You sound like you're proud of it."

He shrugged. "It's just the way the world works."

"No. Not always. Sometimes—"

He didn't let her finish. "Sophie, you're an innocent." He touched her cheek. It was soft and warm as a peach in the sun. She held very still. She *endured* his caress. He dropped his hand away, stepped back just a fraction. "It's the way *my* world works."

"But not mine."

"My point exactly. Your world and my world. Night and day. Shadow and light. They don't exist in the same space. They never have and they never will."

"People *can* change, Sinclair."

"Please. Call me Sin. Everyone does—and do you want to hear the rest or not?"

She drew her shoulders back again. "Yes. All right. Tell me the rest."

He began where he'd left off. "Here, it would have started with a fence."

She frowned. "A fence?"

"Around the five acres you're leasing, to keep you and all your guests off the rest of my land. You see, I know you depend on the use of the whole ranch, to make sure those horses you board get the exercise their owners pay you for.

"Second, I would have built another house. Right on the other side of that fence I just mentioned. Construction can be so *loud*, Sophie. Your guests wouldn't have liked it at all.

"And then, there's this 'theater' of yours. I believe certain zoning regulations are being stretched here. I would have made sure those regulations were strictly enforced—" he gestured at the battered seats, the torn theater screen "—which would have shut this part of your operation down, I'm afraid.

"And do you know what it's like to have the health department after you? To have inspectors paying you regular visits, harassing Myra in her run-down kitchen, just on the off chance that your facilities aren't as *clean* as they ought to be? And what about that damn campground? I know that some of the kids you let stay there have to be runaways. And who knows what they're carrying in those dirty bedrolls. I would have had the police on them, shaking them down. You would have taken some heat, I'm afraid, if any of them were underage or carrying drugs."

She fidgeted, making the folding chair creak. And once again, she couldn't stop herself from defending him. "But, Sin, you didn't do any of those things. You didn't do anything at all, except share five perfect nights with me."

"Sophie. The point is, I have done all those things before. And I would do them to you. If you refused my offer. Because that's who I am, Sophie. That's how I operate. It's all strictly legal. It's all aboveboard. It's what I have every right to do. But what someone like *you* would never do. Because you've got too damn much heart."

"But...you've changed. If you *were* like that, you're not like that anymore."

"Sophie. You are impossible. Not only an innocent, but a romantic, as well. I'm the same man I always was. And whatever this thing is between us, it couldn't last. Frankly, as a general rule, innocence bores me. And romance, as far as I'm concerned, is for starry-eyed fools."

Sophie stared up at him. She yearned to keep arguing with him, keep on defending him.

But it was painfully clear he didn't want to be defended.

And her doubts kept crowding in, reminding her that he had never once said he loved her, though she'd declared her own love repeatedly. That he really had lied to her from the very first.

Five whole days. That was the simple truth. Five whole days in which he had constantly misled her, in which he hadn't uttered a single word about his real aim in coming to the Mountain Star.

Sin could see those doubts in her eyes. He understood that he had lost her—and knew that it was no more than he deserved. "Listen," he heard himself say. "I have a deal for you."

Sophie closed her eyes. He could see it was all too much for her. She needed time to absorb what he'd told her, time to figure out what to do.

He gave her no time. "Sophie, look at me."

She opened her eyes. He had never seen her look so weary. "What deal?"

"You stay current on your lease and things will go on here just as they have been. You can pass out free lunches for the next decade—and more. I'll see to it." The words came out of his mouth without him even knowing he would say them. But once they were out, he knew he would abide by them. "Goodbye, Sophie."

He turned on his heel and headed for the door. Behind him, he heard her cry out softly, "Wait…"

He paused, fool that he was, and turned around again. She had risen to her feet.

She took a step toward him. "Tonight. We were going to talk tonight. Would you have told me all this then?"

The fool inside him sang out, Yes! Everything. I meant to tell it all.

Sin ordered the fool to silence, and asked coldly, "What does it matter?"

"I…it would be something."

"Innocent," he said, infusing the word with all the considerable cynicism at his command. "That's what you are."

"Please. I just want to know. Did you plan to tell me tonight?"

He hesitated on the verge of the truth, but finally answered, "No." Another lie. The kindest one, really.

After all, he had planned to get rid of her. And then, once he'd met her, over and over he had planned to tell her the truth. He had never done either. So what did his intentions really mean in the end?

Nothing. Nothing at all.

She caught her lower lip between her teeth. ''Oh.'' Her whole sweet body seemed to droop. ''I see.''

He turned again. And went through the curtain, the desperate fool inside him hoping against hope that she'd call him back once more.

But she said nothing. And so he kept on walking, across the plank floor of her makeshift lobby and out the open barn doors.

Back where he'd left her, Sophie stood listening. She heard Sin's footsteps retreating. And then she heard nothing except the birds singing outside, and that pigeon she could never get rid of, suddenly taking flight up there in the rafters over her head.

She remembered the projector.

She'd been trying to fix it.

She turned and went to the ladder, started to climb. Halfway up, she stopped. She wanted to be outside. She *needed* to be outside. The projector would just have to wait.

Carefully, she descended. She felt so…slow suddenly. Like someone trying to walk through deep water. Or someone very old and frail.

Outside, the sun shone down and a gentle breeze stirred the pines, making them whisper and sigh to each other, a sound she'd always loved, a sound that had always created a sensation of lightness inside her.

Now she didn't feel light. She felt heavy. Numb.

She walked under the rows of maples, past the stables. Skirting the lawns of the main house, she moved into the shadows of the oak grove, passing through it and then out—across the open pasture, and down to the creek. To the special place. *Their* special place, hers and Sinclair's.

Sin.

He had told her to call him Sin.

"I don't know you," he'd said that first night.

"You know me," she had replied. And he had. He had known so much about her. He had *paid* to learn about her; he'd had her followed for six weeks. Someone had been watching her. Some detective, keeping tabs on her, recording all the details of her life.

Sophie shivered at the thought. She sat on that big dark rock that stuck out into the stream—the rock on which he had kissed her, where she had pleaded with him to come to her bed—and she shivered through her numbness.

"You know me," she had told him.

And he had.

It was she who had not known him.

And that woman. That awful, cold woman: Willa Tweed.

Sin had said he didn't love that woman. Yet he had once meant to marry her. They must have shared something together—desire, perhaps. No doubt Sin must have wanted Willa Tweed once.

Just as he had wanted Sophie.

Sophie rubbed her hands down her shivery arms. Romantic, he had called her. As if it were an insult. And an innocent.

Well, maybe she was. An innocent romantic.

But surely, after what had happened today, she'd never be quite so naive or sentimental again.

She'd been right to let him go, she was sure of it. Because *he'd* been right. In the end, they were much too different from each other. It couldn't have lasted.

She understood that now.

He had said she could keep the Mountain Star.

Could she really believe that?

Time would tell. She'd go on as she always had. And if he came back with his offer to buy out her lease, well, she'd deal with that when the time came. At least now she understood completely what would happen if she refused.

Sophie lay back on the rock. It was a hard bed, but she didn't expect comfort right then. She closed her eyes, listened to the water rushing, the birds singing their midday songs, and wished she could just stay numb forever.

Because she had a terrible feeling that when the numbness passed, the pain of her heart breaking would be impossible to bear.

Chapter Eleven

Her arms full of last night's sheets, Sophie descended the back stairs. She went straight to the pantry area, which also did duty as a laundry room. She set the sheets on the dryer, put detergent in the washer, and then loaded the sheets in on top. She started the cycle and closed the lid.

Upstairs, Midge was supposed to be making up the last of the beds. Sophie knew she ought to trudge back up there and make certain that Midge kept on task. So far that morning, the maid had been utterly useless.

It was a matter of love over duty. Last night, Midge's boyfriend had finally proposed and Midge had accepted. So today, the maid had her mind on wedding announcements and not on getting the beds made.

Sophie started for the stairs again, then stopped

when she got to the base of them. She looked up the narrow, dim stairwell—and remembered.

That first night. Sinclair so grim and distracted as she showed him the lower floor. And then, on those very stairs, grabbing for her, burying his face in her hair. And herself, holding on, promising him that it would be all right....

Sophie closed her eyes in a vain attempt to block out the memory. She turned from the stairwell. Midge was happy. Happiness was rare enough in life. If the beds at the Mountain Star didn't get made until later than usual today, it wouldn't be the end of the world.

Really, Sophie knew she ought to go back over to her office in the spare room of the guest house. She ought to boot up her trusty old Macintosh and balance the accounts.

She ought to. And she would. In a few minutes.

She wandered toward the kitchen. Myra was making her famous blackberry jam today. The smell of the cooking berries hung sweet and heavy in the air. Sophie followed that late-summer scent.

When she reached the doorway, she saw Myra over at the stove, stirring a big, steaming kettle. Caleb stood beside her.

"What's wrong with her?" Caleb spoke quietly—a man who didn't want to be overheard. "She hasn't been herself for three or four days now."

Myra went on stirring. "Since *he* stopped coming round—have you noticed?"

"I noticed." Now Caleb sounded grim. "He's run out on her, hasn't he?"

"She's not talking."

"I'd like to talk to *him*."

Sophie spoke up then, her tone falsely bright. "Please, don't even think about it."

Both of her employees whipped around. "Sophie B.," they muttered in unison. She would have smiled at their guilty expressions—if she'd been in a smiling mood.

"We were just..." Myra hesitated, then finished rather lamely, "...worried about you."

"Don't be. I'm fine."

Caleb jumped in. "That's not true. We all know it's not. You drag around here lookin' miserable. We just want to help."

Sophie waved a hand in front of her face. "There's nothing you can do. Honestly. I will be fine. In a while."

Caleb fisted both big hands. "Just give me that bastard's phone number. It's all I want."

"Caleb, stop it."

"You let me at him."

"Caleb. Listen. It's nothing you can do anything about. Leave it alone."

Myra laid her freckled hand on Caleb's arm. "She's right. It's not for you to settle."

Caleb muttered something truculent, pulled out from under Myra's steadying grip and stalked out. Myra turned back to her cooking blackberries. Sophie dared to come forward, into the room.

"Caleb only wants to make things right," Myra said carefully.

"I know. But there really is nothing he can do."

"He knows that, too. But he doesn't like it one bit." The cook tapped the spoon on the edge of the pot. "And neither do I."

"I will be all right." Sophie uttered the words way too grimly.

"Sure you will." Myra shot her a determined smile, then gestured toward the big table in the center of the room. "Now, bring me that tray of sterilized Mason jars."

The days passed. Sophie went through all the motions that equaled her life. But the joy, the pleasure, seemed leached from it all. Her world had a dullness to it now. It wasn't the way she'd expected to feel. She kept waiting for the real pain of loss to begin, for her heart to break—or else to feel better. Neither seemed to happen. One bleak day passed like the one before it.

Sinclair never tried to contact her. She mailed off the lease payment. And by the time Labor Day had come and gone, she started to believe he must have meant what he said: if she paid her lease on time, she could keep the Mountain Star.

That realization should have helped, shouldn't it? But somehow, it didn't. Except to make her feel angry beneath the dullness.

As if he had bested her somehow. Outdone her in goodness, when he was the one who was supposed to be bad.

Sometimes, at night, she would wake from sensual dreams of him. She would look out the window at the star-thick Sierra sky, wishing he was there beside her, to caress and kiss her, to ease the ache of wanting him.

She almost hated him then, for the way her own body betrayed her. She wanted to forget him, to stop remembering, stop yearning.

To reclaim her life again, the way it used to be, before she had ever laid eyes on him. To return to the time of her own innocence—yes, that was it. To the time when she trusted without question, when she gave without thought of the price it might cost her somewhere down the line.

Going through the motions. Yes, that was her life now. She still did the things she believed in: the campground remained open; Myra continued to give away food they probably should have saved for the paying customers. Midge quit and Sophie immediately hired someone even more hopeless, a four-months' pregnant, unmarried nineteen-year-old named Bethy, whose boyfriend had recently taken off for parts unknown.

Bethy was plagued by continuing morning sickness, which seemed to strike about an hour into her shift. Then she'd have to sit down and chew soda crackers—or simply head home to the house she shared with an older sister and the sister's family. That would leave Sophie making beds, washing sheets, sweeping floors—and resenting it mightily.

Sophie knew that she ought to let Bethy go. And that depressed her further. The girl did need the job. But even Sophie couldn't justify having someone on her limited payroll who never managed to get any work done.

Worst of all, to Sophie's mind, her theater had stopped giving her pleasure. By the weekend after Labor Day, she was showing the fifth installment in her Randi Wilding Retrospective. It was one of Randi's very best films, *Shadowed Heart*. The actress played a retarded woman who managed to show a whole town the real meaning of love and sacrifice.

Sophie had been preparing her introduction to that one for a long time. And then, on Wednesday, September third, Randi Wilding died in a plane crash. The news was all over the papers. It was something Sophie would have cried over once: all that talent and beauty, snuffed out forever. Yet when she heard the news, she felt nothing at all.

She stayed up late into the night, reworking her introductory speech, trying to put into it all the emotions she couldn't make herself feel.

When Thursday night came, the theater was packed. Sophie had to use all of her old folding chairs to seat everyone.

And then, when she got up there in front of them all, her much-rehearsed speech came out sounding utterly flat, totally empty of warmth and compassion. Her audience watched her politely. Some, the ones who visited often, stared with puzzled, slightly worried expressions. In the end, grasping at straws, she threw in a few jokes about the pigeon in the rafters. No one so much as chuckled. She felt only relief when she finally headed for the hayloft to get the darn thing rolling.

Oggie Jones, whom she hadn't seen since she and Sin visited North Magdalene together, showed up on Friday night. When she sold him his ticket, he asked her how she was doing. She pasted on a smile, and chirped out, "Just fine."

He leaned toward her, narrowing his eyes. "You don't look so fine. How's that man of yours?"

A tiny flame of anger licked up inside her. She was getting so tired of having people tell her she didn't look fine, and she didn't need old Oggie Jones asking her about Sin. She did not need that at all.

"I have no *man,* thank you." She shoved his change at him. "And, for your information, I meant what I said. I really am *fine.*"

"Well, pardon me for givin' a damn," the old man growled.

Tears of confusion and shame stung the back of Sophie's throat. Oh, what was *wrong* with her, to speak so sharply to dear Uncle Oggie? She wanted to tell him she was sorry, ask him to please forgive her for behaving so badly. But he was already gone, toddling on that manzanita cane of his toward the open barn doors. She turned a quivery smile on her next customer, promising herself that she would smooth things over after the show.

But then, all through her lifeless introduction, she kept feeling the watchful weight of that beady dark gaze on her. It was nearly as unsettling—though in a totally different way—as the first night Sin had sat in her audience and listened to her opening speech. She had the very unpleasant feeling that Oggie would not let her simply apologize for her rude behavior and be done with it. He was going to bring up the subject of Sin again, she just knew it. And she didn't want to deal with that, not tonight. Not at all.

At intermission, he made things worse. He hobbled up to the concession stand and ordered exactly what Sin had ordered that first night.

"Gimme a bowl of popcorn—and maybe some bottled spring water. Yeah, that sounds refreshin', don't you think, gal?"

She gaped at him. Oggie *never* bought anything at intermission but coffee, light and sweet.

He let out one of those cackling laughs of his. She'd always thought that laugh charming and folksy.

Tonight, it just set her nerves jangling like loose pennies in a rolling jar.

"Come on, popcorn and bottled water. Snap it up, now."

She shoveled the popcorn into a bowl and gave him the water. He made a big show of counting out exact change. Then he said, "You know, gal, with this cane and all, I don't believe I can carry both the bowl and the bottle. I think you're gonna have to help me back to my seat."

There were five other customers waiting behind him. Sophie cast them a rueful glance, half hoping that one of them would either complain—or volunteer to help dear old Uncle Oggie themselves. But this was the Mountain Star, so they all smiled in tolerant understanding.

One of them spoke up. "You go ahead, Sophie B. We can wait."

Oggie chortled away. "Yeah, they can wait." He flung out a hand, indicating the water and popcorn. "Let's move." He turned and started for the open curtains to the main theater, looking way too happy with himself.

Sophie was forced to pick up his refreshments and follow in his wake.

At his seat—on the aisle, thank heaven—he had to make a big event out of laying his cane down just so and settling himself in. Then he winked at her. "Hand 'em over, gal." She passed him the bowl and the bottle of water. "Thank you," he said, nodding his grizzled head like some backwoods potentate. "I surely do appreciate your kindness to an old man." His tiny eyes twinkled merrily.

She gritted her teeth together and kept on smiling,

wishing with all her heart by then that she didn't owe
him an apology.

Shadowed Heart was a real ten-hankie tearfest. By
the time the final credits rolled, all the women were
sobbing and the men kept surreptitiously swiping at
their eyes. Sophie stood by the door as she always
did, saying her farewells—farewells that had become
a bit perfunctory of late.

Her guests lined up, still dabbing at stray tears. All
except Oggie Jones. He stumped right over to the concession counter, where he made a major production
of leaning lazily, looking like a doddery imitation of
Sin on that first night.

Sophie could easily have wrung his wrinkled neck.

Finally, when everyone else was gone, she turned
on him. "What do you think you're doing?"

He grinned. "Waitin' for my chance to find out
what the hell's gone wrong with you."

She glared at him, longing to confront him with his
cruel behavior, especially those petty impersonations
of Sin. But if she did that, she'd only be introducing
the subject she refused to discuss. Finally she settled
for insisting, "There is nothing wrong with me."

He snorted. "Liar."

She felt as if he'd slapped her. And she longed to
slap right back.

In an effort to get control of herself, she turned and
scooped up an armful of empty popcorn bowls. When
she faced him again, she managed to mutter tightly,
"All right. I want you to know I'm sorry for the way
I snapped at you when you bought your ticket."

"Eh? Sorry, are you?"

"Yes. And now I really must ask you to leave. I
have work to do."

"I'm goin' nowhere."

"Excuse me?"

"I said, I'm goin' nowhere. You and me are gonna have a little talk."

"No, we're not. You're leaving and I'm going to—"

"Put those bowls down."

"I beg your pardon?"

"You heard me. Put 'em down."

"You have no right to tell me what to do."

"Someone's gotta." He hit his cane on the floor. Hard. "Put 'em down."

They scowled at each other. Sophie wanted to scream. And say terrible things. And throw the damn bowls in his mean, wrinkled face.

And then, out of nowhere, her eyes filled up. Her throat burned. She realized she was starting to cry.

Oggie spoke more gently. "That's right. It's okay. Set the bowls down now. And you and me will talk this out."

The tears were flowing down her cheeks by then. With a ragged sigh, she turned and set the bowls back on the table.

"Good." He stumped over to her. "Come on." His voice was so soothing, so gentle and kind. He put an arm around her. "It's okay, gal. We'll go outside. We'll talk this out."

Sophie surrendered, burying her head against his bony shoulder and sobbing out her loss into his frayed white shirt.

They sat out in the middle of the lawn, in the cool darkness, on the edge of the fountain with the laughing little girl.

Oggie produced a handkerchief and Sophie blew her nose and blotted the tears. "You tell your Uncle Oggie now, gal. I've solved worse problems than you could ever dream of, believe you me."

And so, between occasional persistent sobs, blotting her eyes when she had to, Sophie told the old man everything. How she had loved Sinclair and given herself completely to him. And the awful, cruel way that he had betrayed her.

When she was done, they sat there in the darkness for a moment, Sophie and the kind old man, with the fountain gurgling behind them and the crickets singing in the grass.

At last, Oggie shook his head. "So then, I guess you don't really love him after all."

Sophie sniffed. Surely she hadn't heard him correctly. "Wh—what did you say?"

"I said, I guess you don't really love him, after all—right?"

She backed away from him an inch or two and spoke with thoroughly justified indignation. "What are you talking about? Of course I love him."

"Then why did you let him go?"

Sophie gaped. How could he even ask such a thing? "He had a detective follow me. He *lied* to me. He pretended to be what he wasn't. He planned to run me out of here if I didn't sell out to him."

Oggie coughed into his hand. "Right. I get it, now. You love him. But you don't love him *enough*."

Sophie hiccupped a final sob away. She could not believe the gall of this old man. Here she'd poured out her heart to him and he had the nerve to accuse her of not loving enough. "How can you say that?"

"Well, because it's the plain truth. Because if you

loved him enough, you'd be thinking about what he actually *did,* which was to go away and let you have this place, after all.''

''But...'' She said the one word, and then couldn't think of what to say next. Pure outrage had rendered her speechless.

Oggie, however, had plenty to say. ''And while we're on the subject, it's quite a damn deal you got here, gal, I gotta tell you. You lease a few buildings and five acres pretty damn cheap and you——''

That got her mouth working. She demanded, ''How do *you* know what I pay for my lease?''

He waved a hand. ''I'm Oggie Jones. I got my sources.''

''But I...you...''

''Stop your sputterin'. I'm still talkin'. Where was I? Right. You lease five acres for a nice low price— and you get to use the rest of the place like it was your own.''

He had it all wrong. She hastened to set him right. ''The teachers' association that owned it before——''

''Gal. This ain't before. This is now. And now, Sinclair Riker owns this ranch. And except for that five acres you won't let go of, he's got the right to do whatever he damn pleases with it—within the boundaries of the law, of course. And what *does* he do? He leaves the whole shebang to you.''

''He didn't *leave* it to me. He only said——''

''You told me what he said. And it amounts to letting you have this place, to run it the way you want to for as long as you want to. Hell, this Sinclair Riker's a damn hero, if you ask me. And any female worthy of the name Jones would chase him down and tell him so.'' He put up both hands, then. ''I know, I know. You're a generous woman. You help out those in need. Everyone for miles around talks about you. They'll be callin' you *Saint* Sophie B. before too many more years. But it seems to me that you're not so generous when it comes to the man you love." He shook his head. "I am sorry to have to be the one to tell you this, gal. But someone has to. And bein' as how we're family—by name and feelin', if not by blood—it falls to me to give it to you straight. And the straight story is, you're mopin' around now, because deep in your heart, you know you have let your man down."

She gasped. "Let *him* down? No. That's not true. You didn't listen to what I told you. *He* let *me* down. He—"

"Save your excuses for someone who'll buy them. You let that man leave when you should have held on until you could figure a way to work things out. And now you know you gotta go after him. But you're scared to go after him—scared he might turn his back on you now."

"Oh, that is wrong. That is so wrong—"

But Oggie was already grabbing his cane, levering himself to his feet with a grunt.

"Wh-where are you going?"

"Home."

"But..."

"But *what*, gal?"

"You can't just say all these cruel things and then leave."

He chortled quite merrily. "Watch me."

Stunned, furious—and just a little bit afraid that he might be right, Sophie stared after him as he hobbled away.

Chapter Twelve

The next morning, Sophie called LA information. She requested the phone number for a company called Inkerris, Incorporated. A recorded voice came on and gave her the number.

She wrote the number down on a Rolodex card. She didn't plan to use it, she really didn't. Last night, instead of sleeping, she'd thought a lot about what Oggie had said. Maybe the old man had a point in one sense. Sin *had* ended up letting her have the Mountain Star, after all. And she would always be grateful to him for that.

Their relationship—or whatever it had been—was over, though. They were from two different worlds. And now they'd both returned to their real lives.

However, it felt good to know for certain that she could reach Sin if she had to—just in case something important came up concerning the ranch.

Having the number did create a little problem, though. She found that as she went through the day, she just couldn't stop thinking about it. Thinking that she had it. And if she wanted to, she could just pick up the phone and—

On Sunday, she gave in. She called the number. A recorded voice informed her that business hours were Monday through Friday, from nine to five. She hung up, her heart beating too fast and her face burning hot.

Monday morning, she got up early and went out for a long ride. She ended up on that ridge where she'd taken Sin the first day they rode together. She looked out over the sparse pastures and thick pine forests below and thought of what he'd said: the trees needed thinning. They would choke out every meadow if left unchecked. And they created a virtual invitation to a forest fire—especially this time of year, when the weather stayed hot and the grasses were dry and brittle as old paper.

Anger rolled through her, low and insistent, like faraway thunder. She'd always found such pleasure in the sight of those trees. And now, because of *him*, she'd started to see them as a potential problem.

The mare she'd chosen tossed her red mane, eager to be moving again. Sophie kept her in check down the hillside and then let her have her head when they found a clear spot—in the meadow of the wild roses, which also reminded her of Sin.

Everything. *Everything* reminded her of Sin.

Once she'd returned the mare to the stable, unsaddled her and brushed her down, Sophie went back to the guest house to wash up before breakfast.

In the bathroom, she splashed cold water on her

face and reached for a towel. She scrubbed away the water and then looked up, catching her own eyes in the mirror. She frowned at herself.

And then, in the back of her mind, she heard Oggie's voice, from the other night.

"Now you know you gotta go after him. But you're scared to go after him—scared he might turn his back on you now...."

Sophie let out a small cry and threw down the towel.

"Oh, all right," she said to the mirror, as if the old man's face looked out at her instead of her own. "I am. I'm just terrified he won't want me anymore."

She knew what Oggie would say then, "Terrified or not, gal. You still gotta go."

She headed straight for the cottage. She needed breakfast—and to find out if Myra and Caleb could handle things by themselves for a couple of days.

Myra said cautiously, "I believe we could manage. It's after Labor Day. We've even been running with a room or two empty during the week. If Bethy will just hold up her end, I'm sure everything will be fine." Bethy wasn't there that morning; she had Monday and Tuesday off.

Caleb swallowed a bite of sausage and demanded, "What's up?"

Sophie answered patiently, "I just told you. I want to visit Los Angeles for a couple of days."

"What for?"

"It's...personal."

Caleb scowled. "So, that's where he lives."

Myra pretended to clear her throat as she slid a warning glance at Caleb. "Now, don't you worry about things here, Sophie B. We can get by. I'm sure that we can."

Caleb wouldn't be deterred. "Why the hell do you want to see *him?*"

"Because…" I love him, Sophie thought. And I can't spend the rest of my life wondering if he might have loved me, too.

"Because what?" Caleb challenged.

"Because…" she said again, then found herself finishing, "…he owns this ranch now."

Caleb's fork clattered against his plate. Myra gasped.

And Sophie felt even worse. "I know, I should have told you before. I *meant* to tell you before. But lately I've been so…"

"Confused and upset." Myra reached across and patted Sophie's hand. "We do understand."

Caleb wasn't so easily put off. "Wait a minute. You're saying that corporation that bought the ranch is owned by Mr. Sinclair Riker, is that it?"

Sophie nodded. "I'm afraid so."

"You make your lease payments to him."

"In effect, yes."

"He owned this place in August, when he was here, with you."

"Yes. That's right."

"But he sat at this table and *said* he was here to look for property deals. He never said—"

"Caleb. Please. Let me work this out my own way."

"That man is trouble. He's no one for you to be runnin' off to see."

"Please, listen. I appreciate your concern. But this is my problem and I will handle it my own way."

"Has he got plans to try to kick us out?"

"No," she answered quickly, silently adding, Or at least, I don't *think* he does, not anymore....

Caleb made a low, disgusted noise, then stabbed another sausage. "I don't like this, Sophie B."

"But can you—*will you*—take care of things here if I leave for a day or two?"

"Of course we will," said Myra.

Caleb forked up another sausage and sawed it in half before he grudgingly answered, "All right. We'll take care of things."

Back in the guest house, Sophie tried information again, hoping she might discover Sin's home phone number. But there was no listing for a man named Sinclair Riker. So at nine on the nose, she dialed Inkerris, Incorporated. Her hand shook as she punched up the numbers and her voice sounded thin and squeaky when she asked for the address there. The woman on the other end rattled it right off. Sophie had already hung up before it occurred to her that she might simply have asked to speak to Sin.

She punched Redial—and then hung up before it rang.

She was already a nervous wreck about this. She just couldn't afford to be put off by some receptionist. No, she would go down there. All the way to LA. And she wouldn't come back until she'd spoken with Sin face-to-face.

What exactly she would say to him, she hadn't a clue. But she would *see* him. She would *talk* with him. And by the time she came home, she'd have some kind of idea if what they'd shared had been anything more than a beautiful—and ultimately heart-breaking—summer fling.

The next morning, Sophie flew into LAX from Sacramento. She bought a map at the airport and rented a car. Then she fought her way through the awful traffic to the Century City offices of Inkerris, Incorporated.

The sight of the building completely intimidated her. It was a tall, imposing, very modern structure of black marble and glass. She drove by in her small rented car and wondered how she'd ever get up the nerve to go inside, walk up to some security guard and ask to speak to Sinclair Riker.

Oh, Uncle Oggie had been so right. She never should have let Sin leave her side until she was sure he didn't want to try again. Her original cowardice had only made things all the more difficult in the end.

A hotel, she decided. She'd find one first. And then come back and walk through those tall, gleaming glass doors. It was putting off the inevitable, she knew it; more evidence of her own cowardice. But she did it anyway.

She found a room in a small hotel about a mile away from Inkerris, Incorporated. Then she sat on the end of the bed for a while, staring at her own reflection in the mirror over the low chest of drawers and telling herself she had no more excuses now.

It was after three when she finally slipped through the doors of Sin's building. She found herself facing acres of marble floor and two banks of elevators. Over near the far wall was an information desk, with a directory on the wall behind it. She drew her shoulders back and marched over there. The man behind the desk watched her as she approached.

She tried to simply scan the directory over his head, but then he asked, "May I help you?"

She cleared her throat. "I'd like to speak to Sinclair Riker, please."

The man gave her an indifferent smile. "Your name?"

She had to cough again, in a rather futile effort to make her throat relax. "Sophie. Sophie B. Jones."

"Do you have an appointment?"

"Uh…no. No, I don't."

Right then, a phone near his elbow buzzed. He put up an index finger. "Just a minute." Then he picked up the phone. "Lobby. Yes. No. All right." He hung up and looked at Sophie again. "What is your visit concerning?"

Now how could she answer that? She stammered, "I-it's a personal matter."

He looked at her sideways, a look that she read as disapproving—or disbelieving. But then he did pick up the phone and punched a button. "This is Jerry in the lobby. I have a Ms. Jones down here. To see Mr. Riker. She says it's a personal matter." He paused, listened. "Yes. Good enough." He hung up, smiling for the second time, as indifferently as before. "Mr. Riker isn't in. Would you like to leave a number?"

Sophie's heart sank. That was it. She'd been turned away. By Sin himself, possibly. Or maybe not. How could she know? And what in the world was she going to do now? "I…"

Now the man looked impatient. "Just give me a number. I'm sure he'll get back to you."

She drew herself up. "No. Really. I'd like to speak with his...secretary, please."

"Ms. Jones..."

She tried to stand even taller. "Please."

With a shrug, the man picked up the phone again. "This is Jerry downstairs again. Ms. Sophie B. Jones would like to speak with Mr. Riker's secretary, rather than leaving a number here." Jerry listened, looking Sophie over while whoever was on the other end of the line spoke. Though the air conditioning in the building seemed to be set on high, Sophie felt the sweat break out under her arms. At last, he said into the phone, "No, I don't think so." and then, "All right." He hung up, looked at Sophie. "Take the far bank of elevators. Top floor. Penthouse."

She stared, hardly daring to believe she'd actually made progress, no matter how minimal.

"The far bank of elevators," Jerry said again, clearly uncertain whether she'd heard him or not.

She gave him a grateful smile. "Yes. All right. And thank you."

He smiled back, more warmly than before. "You're welcome."

She turned and hurried toward the elevators.

On the top floor, the elevator doors slid open onto a wide reception area. The marble floors were inlaid with diamond patterns. Fabulous Egyptian-design rugs covered parts of that floor, with leather chairs grouped around them. A long desk ran along one wall. Behind that desk sat a gorgeous brunette.

"Ms. Jones?"

"Yes."

"Have a seat. Mr. Taylor will be with you shortly."

Sophie sank into one of the leather chairs to wait. The brunette started typing on her word processor. Sophie's nerves hummed in anticipation and dread. The big room seemed so quiet, except for the brunette, punching the keys: *click-click-click-click.* Sophie hoped it wouldn't be long.

Twenty minutes later, the brunette looked up. "Are you sure you wouldn't rather just leave a number?"

"No," Sophie said. "I'll wait."

And wait she did. For another hour and ten minutes, as the brunette typed away and intermittently answered the phone. Then, near five, the phone buzzed again. The brunette picked it up. "Yes?" The brunette's clear blue eyes met Sophie's—and then she quickly looked away. "No. Not yet," she said gingerly.

Sophie's heart thudded dully in her chest. She just knew it was Sin, asking if she'd given up and left yet. She wanted to jump to her feet and demand that he talk to her. At the same time, she wished she could just sink through that leather chair, down ten floors and right on through the ground all the way to China.

The brunette hung up. "Mr. Taylor will be right out."

Sophie gulped. She didn't know whether to feel relieved or more nervous. "Thank you."

A few moments later, the tall mahogany doors to the left of the brunette's desk swung open. A movie-star-handsome blond man in a suit straight out of *GQ* appeared. He saw Sophie and advanced on her, holding out his hand.

Sophie leapt to her feet.

"Ms. Jones." His hand was cool, firm and dry. Sophie's own hand felt suddenly clammy. She resisted the urge to yank it away and wipe it dry on her skirt.

He let go, granting her a smile as cool as his handshake. "I'm Rob Taylor, Mr. Riker's personal assistant. What can I do for you?"

She put on her best no-nonsense tone. "I'm here to see Mr. Riker."

A tiny frowned creased his tanned brow. "I thought Jerry downstairs told you—"

"That he isn't in. Yes. The man downstairs did tell me that. But I—"

"Ms. Jones." His tone had turned from bland to patronizing. "Really. I'm sorry you insisted on waiting to talk to me. I realize we've wasted too much of your time. But Mr. Riker honestly is not here."

She couldn't just give up now. "When will he be here?"

"Ms. Jones—"

"Tomorrow. In the morning? Is that the best time to—"

"Ms. Jones. Please. Give me your number. I will make certain that he gets it."

Beyond his shoulder, Sophie could see the beautiful brunette. Watching. Probably wondering what was the matter with her, that she had such difficulty taking a hint.

"Ms. Jones, I—"

Sophie sighed. "All right." She had a Mountain Star business card in her purse. She took it out, groped around for a pen, and then scribbled the name of her hotel on the back of it. "I don't know the phone number there offhand. But it's over on—"

Rob Taylor took the card almost before she finished writing on it. He glanced at it. "I know the Helmswood Arms." He gestured at the brunette behind the reception desk. "Tessa can look up the phone number." He took Sophie's arm and herded her toward the elevator doors. "I'll see that Mr. Riker gets your message." He pressed the button and the doors opened. "Have a nice day." He guided her into the car. The doors slid soundlessly shut on his too-handsome face.

Sophie wanted to fling herself at those doors, pound on them, order them to open again. But what good would it do? If she got out of the car, Rob Taylor would probably only shove her back inside again—or call Jerry downstairs and have her bodily removed from the building.

The elevator began going down.

As she descended, Sophie couldn't help thinking that the wisest move now would be to check out of the Helmswood Arms, head to LAX and wait on standby until she could get a flight home. Instead, she returned to her room, took a long, hot shower, put on a clean dress and visited a deli for a ham on rye.

By the time she sat down with her sandwich, she felt marginally better. She had to think positive. After all, it was entirely possible that Rob Taylor had only told the truth: Sin simply hadn't been there.

Maybe she was whistling at the moon, but she would give it—give Sin—another twenty-four hours. Her flight back was scheduled for tomorrow evening. She could keep trying until then. Maybe he would call. And if he didn't, she'd gather all her courage up and storm the gates of Inkerris, Incorporated, one more time.

Sophie consumed all of her sandwich, a large glass of milk and both of the big slices of dill pickle that came with it. As she ate, she plotted her next attack on the marble and glass bastions of Inkerris, Incorporated.

Tomorrow, if Sin hadn't called, she would try a different approach. This time, she'd go in as the owner-operator of the Mountain Star, a tenant of Inkerris, Incorporated. She'd tell Mr. Taylor that she simply had to see Mr. Riker concerning the property she leased from him.

It might not work any better than citing ''personal'' reasons had. But it certainly couldn't do any worse.

By the time she got back to her room after visiting the deli, she'd almost convinced herself that the message light on the phone would be blinking. It wasn't.

She told herself she would not become discouraged.

However, she just might go nuts if she sat in that room all evening, staring at the four walls. LA was full of small movie theaters, the kinds of places that showed movies only someone like Sophie would enjoy.

She got an *LA Times* and chose a place that was showing *It Came from Outer Space* and *Attack of the Killer Tomatoes*. She ate bad popcorn, drank flat root beer and laughed at awful dialogue. By eleven, when the show was over and she emerged into the balmy LA night, she almost felt good.

But back at the hotel, the message light remained dark. She hardly slept the whole night, her nerves on a razor's edge, waiting for the phone to ring.

It never did.

The next morning she rose at six. She took a long

walk down city streets that were already clogging up with cars. Around eight, she stopped for breakfast at an outdoor café. She ate croissants and poached eggs, sitting next to a potted palm beneath a Cinzano umbrella. Then she returned to her room—to find she had no messages.

She waited until nine-thirty. And then she grabbed her purse and headed for Inkerris, Incorporated, one more time.

Sin stared out the window behind his desk at the spectacular view of Century City as Rob Taylor filled him in on yesterday's messages and today's appointments.

"Oh, and I almost forgot," Rob said when the endless list had seemed to be finished. "Some young woman came to see you." Rob sighed, sounding put-upon. "She was very persistent. A Ms. Jones. Ms. Sophie B. Jones."

Sin spun his chair around. "When was she here?"

Rob blinked. "Yesterday. In the afternoon. She—"

"Did she leave a number?"

Rob fell back a step. "Well, yes. That is, she left a card, with the name of her—"

"Give it to me."

"I—"

"You do have it?"

"Yes. Of course. That is, I gave it to Tessa to look up the number."

"What number?"

"The number of her hotel."

"What hotel?"

"Helmswood Arms, I believe."

Sin grabbed the phone and buzzed the receptionist.

Rob kept babbling. "Honestly. If I had known—"

He waved his assistant to silence. "Tessa, do you have the number of that hotel where Sophie Jones is staying?"

"Of course, Mr. Riker. Just a minute." Sin waited, glaring at Rob, wanting to scream at poor Tessa to snap it up. Finally she spoke again. "Here it is. Shall I call it for—"

"No. Give it to me."

"Certainly. 555-3072."

He disconnected Tessa and punched up the number, growling Sophie's name as soon as a voice said, "Helmswood Arms."

"One moment, please." He heard a line ringing. Five rings, and then the hotel operator came back on. "I'm sorry. She's not answering. Would you care to—"

"What's your address there?" He grabbed a pen and scribbled it down, then slammed the phone back in its cradle and once more turned his attention on the hapless Rob. "I'm going over there. Now."

"Yes. Of course. Whatever."

"If she comes back here, you ask her to wait and you have me paged at her hotel. Is that clear?"

"Yes. Perfectly."

Sin was already striding for the door. He paused only to bark over his shoulder. "I mean it, Rob. Give her coffee. Give her caviar. Give her whatever the hell she wants. But if she comes here, do not let her go until I get back."

Rob was still swearing he'd handle everything as Sin slammed out the door.

Sophie entered the lobby of Inkerris, Incorporated, at nine-forty-five. This time, she had sense enough to head straight for the elevators before Jerry, behind the information desk, caught so much as a glimpse of her. The lobby was busier that time of day than it had been the afternoon before. The up light was already on. She waited with several preoccupied-looking button-down types for the mirrored doors to slide open.

When they finally did, Sin was standing inside.

Sophie's heart went racing. Her feet felt cold and her face felt hot. Neither she nor Sin moved an inch as the button-down types bustled around them, getting on and off the elevator car.

A thousand unreconciled emotions did battle inside her. He looked so unbelievably handsome, more handsome than she remembered, if that was possible. And he was so perfectly dressed, in a dark gray silk suit and a blue shirt and a tie of some deep, rich indefinable color between blue and black.

He looked…urbane and sophisticated. And certainly not the kind of man who could be interested in her, not in a hundred thousand years.

Oh, what had possessed her to come here? They'd shared five days—or, more specifically, five magical nights.

But looking at him now, here in the marble and glass confines of his own world, she just couldn't believe that those days and nights had meant anything near as much to him as they had to her.

Just then the doors started to close.

Sin shouted, "Hold that door!"

But it was too late. The doors kept on sliding together. He commanded, "Sophie. Stay there." And then the doors shut all the way, with him inside—and her still standing there, staring at the place where he had been.

"Stay there," he had said.

She supposed he meant he would come back down on the next car. She *hoped* that was what he meant. Or maybe he had meant, stay there—and away from me.

Well, it didn't matter. Laying eyes on him again had left her feeling a little unsteady, anyway. Staying there for a while would suit her fine.

A small marble bench stood against the section of wall between the two banks of elevators. Sophie stumbled over and dropped down onto it.

The seconds ticked by like centuries. At last Sin's elevator car descended again, the doors opened, and he stepped out. Sophie stood from the bench. He turned and saw her there.

For a moment, when his eyes met hers, she thought everything would be all right after all. They would run to each other across the black marble floor. He would sweep her into his arms. All their differences would simply melt away....

For his part, at that moment, Sin felt exactly the same.

But then skepticism took over.

There might be any number of reasons she had come here to find him. He decided he'd be wise to approach her carefully until he understood better what was really going on.

As Sin decided to proceed with caution, Sophie felt the moment of hope fade away. Once again, he was simply that incredibly handsome, sophisticated stranger who couldn't possibly be interested in someone like her.

He started toward her, his stride purposeful and his eyes wary. She had no idea what he intended to do, until he reached her and held out his hand.

"How are you, Sophie?"

They shook. Like two casual acquaintances. She felt his touch all the way to her toes, at the same time as she made her lips turn up in a polite smile that pretended she didn't feel anything at all.

"I'm doing all right. How about you?"

He shrugged and, to her sincere regret, released her hand. "I'm all right, too." Behind him, the button-down types came and went from the elevator cars. "I meant what I said, Sophie." He had lowered his voice a little. "I won't take your Mountain Star."

She looked at him levelly. "Yes. I...believe that now."

"Then what brings you here?"

I love you, and I want you to come back to me! her heart cried. But how could she blurt that out here, by the elevators, with all those busy people milling around a few feet away?

"Is there a problem at the ranch?"

She hesitated, her mind all caught up in what she longed to say, what she was afraid to say. "A...problem?"

"Something you came to see me about?"

Now it seemed to her that some of the button-down types were beginning to stare. "I wonder...could we go somewhere a little more private, do you think?"

"Of course." He started to reach for her hand— she could have sworn that he did. But then he only touched her on the shoulder. "Come with me." He turned for the elevators again. She followed after him.

They got on the elevator with two young, well-dressed women. "Good morning, Mr. Riker," the women chirped, almost in unison.

"Good morning, Sarah. Danielle." He nodded, so

polite, so correct. A king dispensing the favor of his attention on his subjects.

Sarah and Danielle got off on the fifth floor. Sin and Sophie rode the rest of the way up in an awkward silence that made the close space seem way too small.

It was a relief when the doors opened onto the penthouse reception area.

Tessa looked up from her keyboard. She smiled.

"We'll be in the west conference room." Sin put his hand at the small of Sophie's back, causing the skin there, even beneath the layers of clothing, to burn—making her whole body tighten and yearn. "See that we aren't disturbed."

"I'll do that," Tessa promised.

Sin looked at Sophie. "Can I have Tessa bring you anything?"

She wished he'd take his hand away—she wished he'd never let go. "Anything?" she repeated idiotically.

"Coffee? A sweet roll?"

"Coffee," she said automatically, because it seemed like something she ought to say, though she'd had two cups at breakfast and that was more than enough.

"I'll bring it right in," Tessa promised.

Sin exerted the slightest pressure on Sophie's back—guiding her forward toward the tall mahogany doors. Once through them, they went down a wood-paneled hallway to another pair of double doors. He ushered her through.

The room they entered had a huge, diamond-shaped table in the center of it, with leather chairs all around. There were three sofas along the walls, and chairs and low tables grouped around them—for more informal meetings, she supposed. One wall was solid glass. It afforded a panoramic view of the well-groomed Century City streets below.

Sin guided her to a sofa and chairs near that wall of glass. "Have a seat."

Really, she wanted to stand. She had such a strong feeling of unreality about all of this. She'd come to talk of love—and here they were about to have what felt like some sort of business meeting. Still, to remain on her feet would only make her look as apprehensive as she felt. She dropped into one of the chairs.

Just then a small door down at the other end of the room opened. Tessa came in, carrying a coffee service on a black lacquer tray. She hurried over and set it on a low table about a foot from where Sophie sat perched on her chair.

Efficiently, Tessa poured. She arched a brow at Sophie. "Sugar? Cream?"

"No, black is fine."

She passed Sophie the cup and saucer, which started rattling the moment Sophie got them in her hand. She slid them onto the table in front of her, stifling a sigh of relief when the clattering stopped.

"Mr. Riker?" Tessa held up the pot for him.

"No, thanks. That's all, Tessa."

Tessa set down the pot and left them alone.

Sin was still standing, leaning a little against a credenza not far from the sofa. Sophie felt a flash of resentment. He'd asked her to sit. And yet he remained in the superior position on his feet, looming over her.

"You're not drinking your coffee," he remarked quietly.

She reached out, plucked the cup from the saucer

and took a sip that burned the back of her throat when she swallowed. Somehow she managed not to completely humiliate herself by having a choking fit right there in front of him.

She set the cup down.

He crossed his arms over his chest.

And she remembered that first night—the two of them, standing by the twin sinks in the back room of her barn-theater. He had leaned against the sink then, just exactly as he leaned against that credenza now....

"What is it, Sophie? What can I do for you?"

She thought, I love you. Do you love me?

But she couldn't say it. She didn't know *how* to say it. Not anymore. Not here, not now. Not to this urbane, sophisticated man. And not in the west conference room on the penthouse floor.

"Sophie?" He looked puzzled—and maybe a little concerned. "Please. Tell me what's on your mind."

And she heard herself announcing, "Listen, I have a deal for you."

She waited for him to laugh out loud.

But instead, he lifted a dark brow and actually looked interested. "Oh, really?"

"Yes. Really. I wonder, would you consider becoming my partner in the Mountain Star?"

Chapter Thirteen

Sophie could not believe she had said that—but now that it was out, she decided she would just go with it. Until he turned her down, which he surely would. Then she could slink away like the complete coward she was.

He was watching her, the consummate business-man, revealing nothing, willing to let her play her whole hand. She picked up her coffee cup, took a second, much more careful sip, and set it back down. "I mean, I understood you had planned to live there anyway, right? Back when you were..." How to say it diplomatically? "...hoping to convince me to give up my lease?"

"Yes," he agreed, looking reasonably serious, as if he actually were considering this outrageous "deal" she was making up as she went along. "That was my plan."

"So, that would mean that you must have your affairs pretty much in order here." At the word *affairs,* she thought of Willa Tweed and had to hold back a slightly hysterical laugh.

Sin wasn't thinking of Willa at all.

He said, "That's true."

And it was. Since he'd left Nevada County—and Sophie—Sin had been trying to figure out what the hell to do next. Inkerris, Incorporated, was now virtually run by his former second-in-command, who had plans to buy Sin out completely within the next couple of years. In the past few weeks, since his return, Sin hadn't bothered to change those plans. He had realized he was ready to move on to something different.

But a partnership with Sophie? She couldn't be serious. And *he* had to be losing his mind to even consider such a suggestion. He had wanted the ranch to himself. That had been the whole point.

She forged ahead. "What I've been thinking is, well, maybe we could work out a way that we both end up getting what we want."

He prodded her on. "And what way is that?"

"Well, as I said, I was thinking of kind of a..." She gulped, as if the next word had gotten stuck in her throat.

He helped her with it. "A partnership, you said. A partnership between you and me."

"Yes. That's what I said. Is that crazy?"

"Well..."

"You think it's crazy."

"Sophie, I didn't say that."

She went for broke. "You know how you were always saying you'd like to build yourself another house? Well, you could do that. You could. Remember that meadow, the one with the wild roses?''

He nodded.

''Well, that would be a beautiful place for a house. And it's over that little hill from the other buildings. So the construction noise shouldn't carry too badly.''

The developer inside him immediately began thinking of access roads, of septic systems, of getting power out there. But none of that should be too much of a problem. It wasn't that far away from the other buildings, or from paved road. And the meadow she referred to *was* beautiful.

She was frowning. ''Maybe you don't like that spot.''

''No. I like it. It's a beautiful spot.''

''But you don't want to do it.''

''I didn't say that.''

''But I—''

''Sophie, exactly what do you mean by a partnership?''

''Well, maybe you don't want a partnership.''

''I didn't say that. I asked what kind of a partnership you're talking about.''

It was clear from the dazed look on her face that she hadn't the faintest idea.

He heard himself suggesting for her, ''You could use an investor more than a partner.''

''Uh…tell me more.''

''Someone who would finance the improvements you need—Myra's new kitchen, a new projector for that theater of yours.…''

''You mean, I would still run things and you'd take a percentage of the profits in exchange for putting money into the Mountain Star?''

"That's the general idea."

She scrunched up her sweet face.

"What?" he demanded. "What are you thinking?"

"Well, Sin, you have to know that there aren't really enough profits to get excited about."

Yet he *was* getting excited. "There could be profits. If you added on to the main house, so that you wouldn't have to turn people away in the busy season. And if you expanded the stables and hired men to work with Caleb, so you could enlarge that boarding service of yours."

She murmured faintly, "Add on to the main house? Expand the stables?"

He backed off a little. "We wouldn't have to do everything right away. We could...take it slow. Fix the kitchen, buy that projector..."

"Yes, yes, of course we could." Now she was sitting forward on the edge of her chair, her chin tipped up and her hands folded in her lap. Sin thought he'd never seen such an enchanting sight.

But go into partnership with her? It could never work.

Then again, why in hell would she offer such a thing—unless she had hopes that the two of them might rediscover what they'd lost?

Which they couldn't, of course. They were miles apart now—if they ever really had been that close.

But still, he might be of use to her. At the very least he should be able to get her to fix up that damn kitchen and put a new roof on the main house.

Take it slow. That was the best way. "Maybe I should come up there—for a few days or a week. Nothing formal, right now."

She looked more confused than ever. "Nothing formal?"

"I mean, we won't actually form a legal partnership yet. Nothing on paper. I'll just come and stay for a while. We'll really look into what needs to be done around there. And I'll check into your idea of building a house in that meadow you mentioned."

A few days or a week, Sophie thought. It wasn't a bad idea. Surely in that time, they could begin to find their way back to each other—or she could start learning to accept that it hadn't worked out.

He was saying, "We could see how well we work together. How we...get along. What would you say to something like that?"

She hardly knew what to say. It wasn't exactly what she'd come here for. But it was a whole lot better than nothing. She put on a bright smile. "I think it's a great idea. When can you come?"

"I have a few things to wrap up here. But I could manage to get away by next Monday, say? What do you think?"

"I think that would be just fine."

"Great then. We're agreed."

"Yes. Agreed." It seemed like one of those times a person should offer to shake hands, so Sophie popped out of her chair and extended her arm. They shook, as they had down in the lobby. Her palm burned, pressed so close to his. She thought of their nights together, of the way they always slept with their legs intertwined, of waking in the morning to find herself all wrapped up with him, so close she could hardly tell where her body ended and his began.

He let go of her hand. They stared at each other.

She edged back a few steps. "Well, I know you have work to do and so I suppose I'd better—"

"How about lunch?"

"Lunch?" She said the word as if she'd never heard it before—and then felt her face grow warm.

He smiled that almost smile she remembered so well. "I'll pick you up at noon. At your hotel. How's that?"

"My hotel?" she echoed numbly.

"The Helmswood Arms, is that right?"

"Uh, yes. The Helmswood Arms."

"At noon, then?"

"Well, that would be…yes. That would be nice."

Oh, it felt lovely, just to sit across from him, to look at him, to hear his voice.

But never once during the lunch they shared did he say anything about the two of them, about all that had happened between them less than a month before. Not that she could blame him for that. She said nothing either.

And she was the one who had come to see *him*.

It just…all felt so different now, between them. Careful. Cordial. And distant.

Before, when he'd appeared at her theater and swept her off her feet, it had been so perfect, so natural. So right. The idea of hesitating to reach out, to touch him, had never even occurred to her then. He'd owned her heart that first night. And by the second night, he'd shared her bed. It had been pure magic, the instant connection between them.

Now she still felt the yearning. The need to get closer.

But she didn't know how to go about it anymore.

It was as if loving him was a special skill she'd mastered once on the first try.

And now somehow she'd fallen out of practice. She'd lost the magic touch that had brought them together so effortlessly before.

"Innocent," he had called her just before he left her.

And she had been.

Now she was wiser. More guarded. Less willing to risk her wounded heart.

Now she could sit across from him in a restaurant and talk and laugh and never once blurt out, *I love you—do you love me, too?*

They ended up arguing over the bill. She wanted to pay it, he insisted he would take care of it. Then she suggested they split it.

He looked pained. "Don't be ridiculous."

She jumped to her own defense. "I don't think it's ridiculous that I offer to pay half."

He tossed down his platinum American Express card and the waiter swiftly scooped it up. "Sophie. That's not what I meant."

"You said—"

"Sophie." He just looked at her, across the snowy white tablecloth and the little centerpiece of pink roses. "It's taken care of. Let it go."

"But I—"

"Let it go."

She sank back in her chair. He was right. She knew it. It was only lunch, after all. The real problem had more to do with all she'd yet to say to him than who picked up the check. She folded her hands on the table and looked down at them. "I guess I'm…a little nervous about all this."

"Do you want to call it off?"

She snapped her head up and searched his face—for all the good it did. She couldn't for the life of her guess what might be going through his mind.

"I asked if you wanted to call it off."

"No! I mean…just because I'm nervous doesn't mean I've changed my mind."

"You still want me to come stay at the Mountain Star, then?"

"I do."

"You're sure?"

"Positive—but are you sure *you* want to come?"

"I wouldn't have suggested it if I didn't." The waiter returned and set the bill tray down with a flourish. Sin picked up the pen and signed the receipt. "All right," he said, once the waiter was gone again. "So we have a deal—or at least, the beginnings of one."

"Yes. We have a deal."

Sin insisted on taking her back to the Helmswood Arms. Before she got out of the car, he asked when she would be flying home.

"Tonight at six-thirty."

For a moment she could have sworn he was going to suggest she might stay longer. But he didn't. He only wished her a safe flight and promised he'd see her in five days.

She ended up standing on the sidewalk in front of her hotel, watching his long black limousine pull away and drive off.

"Well, I hope you got *that* out of your system," Caleb said when he picked her up at Sacramento International.

Sophie granted him a sour smile. "It's nice to see you, too—and you can stop talking about Sin as if he were some kind of virus."

"*Sin?* Is that what you call him?" Caleb snorted. "It fits."

She waited until they got home and she could get both him and Myra together before she explained that Sin was considering investing in the Mountain Star and possibly building a house nearby.

"He'll be arriving Monday, to stay for a week or so. It will be a sort of…trial period. We'll decide after that if we think a partnership between us might work out."

Caleb let out a short Anglo-Saxon expletive. "I don't get it. I don't get any of it."

Sophie kept her voice low and firm. "Please treat him with courtesy, Caleb."

"Why?"

"Because he is coming here in good faith, he owns the property we're standing on and…because I asked you to."

Caleb muttered more swear words, then demanded, "Did he walk out on you or not?"

"Caleb, please…" Myra chided.

"It's all right, Myra," Sophie said. She faced Caleb. "He did leave, yes. There were…problems between us. And instead of trying to work them out, I just let him go. I shouldn't have done that. That's why I went to find him. And now, we're starting over."

"As *business* partners?"

"Yes, possibly."

"It doesn't make any sense."

"It doesn't *have* to make sense. All I'm asking is, will you treat him with courtesy?"

Caleb glowered.

And Myra spoke up again. "Caleb. This is not our choice to make. And Sophie B. is the boss."

Caleb folded his big arms over his chest.

"Caleb," Sophie murmured softly, "please…"

He grunted. "All right. I don't like it, but you *are* the boss."

Sophie spent the next five days on an emotional pendulum, swinging back and forth between euphoria and dread. She couldn't wait for Sin to come—and she couldn't help wondering what kind of awful mess she might have gotten them into.

On Sunday, remembering how uncomfortable Riker cottage made him, she moved her clothes and a few personal things there, to a small attic room next to Myra's room.

Certainly he'd enjoy the space and privacy of the guest house more. She figured she could still use her office there without inconveniencing him too much, for the original period of time he planned to stay.

After that, who could say? Anything might happen. Maybe they'd be truly together again. Maybe they'd be business partners.

And maybe he'd simply fly back to LA and get on with his own life, leaving her here to get on with hers.

He arrived at eleven-thirty on Monday morning, right when Sophie just happened to be making the bed in one of the rooms that looked out over the front driveway. She ran to the window when she heard the car drive up. At the sight of the shiny black Lexus below, she knew that it had to be him.

She tossed the lace pillows against the headboard and smoothed the quilt one more time. Then she flew out to the hall, raced down the front stairs, flung open the old oak door and rushed outside.

Halfway down the walk, she began to feel foolish, running at him headlong like some eager, impetuous child. She ordered her feet to move at a more sedate pace.

His door opened and he emerged from the car. And Sophie found herself hovering there, at the edge of the walk, clasping her hands together, awkward and shy as a preteen in the grip of a first crush.

"So," she said nervously. "You're here."

"Yes," he concurred. "I am."

They stood there in the late-morning sun just looking at each other—for an embarrassingly long stretch of seconds. Again, she thought it could never work out. He was too handsome, too rich, too…everything.

And they would never get past this awful uneasiness with each other.

Sin was experiencing similar emotions. Those wide eyes regarded him anxiously—as if, now he'd come, she had no idea what to do with him.

Finally he suggested, "I'll just get my suitcase and—"

"No."

What the hell did that mean? Had she changed her mind—and not bothered to call and inform him of the fact?

But then she explained, "I've put you in the guest house. I hope that's…all right."

All right?

Pure elation made Sin's heart do something impossible inside his chest, something that felt like a forward roll.

He could hardly believe it. Here he'd been telling

himself for five days that he had to be crazy to come here, that what had once been was over. And all the time Sophie had intended for him to move back into the guest house with her.

He understood everything, then. Yes, she looked anxious. She was afraid he might say no.

Laughable thought. That he could ever say no to her...

"Sin?" She stared at him, adorably apprehensive. "Will that be all right?"

"That will be just fine."

"Well, then, why don't you just follow the driveway over there?"

He wanted to pull her into his arms right then and there, but he didn't. He could wait—somehow—until they were alone. He suggested, "Come with me."

"Sure." She started to turn, to cut across the lawn.

"Sophie." She stopped, whirled toward him again, her huge eyes questioning. She wore old jeans and a T-shirt with *Mountain Star* emblazoned across the front. Her glorious hair had a ragged-edged scarf tied over it. He couldn't wait to take that scarf off. He gestured at the passenger's side of the Lexus. "Get in."

She waved a hand. "Oh, that's not necessary. I'll just run across the lawn and—"

"Sophie. Get in."

She hesitated a moment more, then she shrugged and went around the front of the Lexus. They settled in next to each other and he drove the short distance to the guest house.

She had her door open again almost before he brought the car to a complete stop. "I'll help you with your things."

"Sophie, that's not necess—"

But she was already halfway around to the back. Shaking his head, he popped the trunk latch.

She had the trunk lid up and was hauling the heavier of his two bags out when he got back there himself. He took the bag away from her and grabbed the garment bag, as well.

"Sin, I don't mind—"

He gave her a look. She stopped protesting in midsentence.

Inside, she led him straight to her bedroom. "Well, here we are." She gestured him through the doorway, lingering on the threshold herself.

Hiding a knowing smile, Sin tossed the garment bag across the bed and set his suitcase on the needlepoint rug. He turned to her.

She was fiddling with that ragged scarf she'd tied over her hair. "I...hope you'll be comfortable here." She threw out a hand toward the bureau. "I cleared out the drawers for you. And there's room in the closet for your other things." She smoothed the scarf, let her hands drop to her side—and then couldn't leave them there. She clasped them nervously together. "I hope you won't mind, if I go ahead and use the office room. But I'll try not to bother you, I promise."

He didn't know what she was babbling about. "Not bother me?"

She rubbed her arms as if the room were cold. "Well, I mean, as much as possible, I'll leave you your privacy."

"My *privacy*."

"Yes. I mean, I'll just use the back door, if that's

all right. And the front of the house will be completely yours.''

Completely mine, he thought, somehow restraining himself from parroting her words for the third time in a row.

It had all come painfully clear.

She wasn't inviting him to share her house at all; she had moved her things elsewhere. He would be staying here alone.

And he knew why she'd done it.

Because *she* knew how he felt about the main house. She'd seen his absurd reaction to it that first night they met.

She knew his ludicrous weakness—and he hated that she knew. It was almost as bad as the other things she knew about him: all his schemes and his lies.

He asked very quietly, ''Where are *you* staying?''

She shrugged, a gesture that was way too offhand. ''There's a cute little room in the main house. I moved my things there.''

''A cute little room that just happens to be up in the attic. Right?''

She shifted her stance. Her gaze slid away, then back. ''Yes. In the attic.''

''One of the two maid's rooms, right? A room nobody wants—unless you're operating at capacity and they can't get anything else.''

She'd stopped shifting from one sneakered foot to the other. Her eyes looked wounded and defiant at once.

He demanded, ''Which one of the maid's rooms is it? The one where my father had the bad taste to hang himself?''

She hiked up her chin. ''No. Not that one.''

"Oh, that's right. That would be the bigger room of the two. I suppose Myra's got that one."

"Sin, why are you—?"

"Answer me. Does Myra have the larger room?"

"Yes. But what does it matter? The two rooms share a *bath*, for heaven's sake. I just…I knew you'd be much more comfortable here."

"I'm sure you did."

"Sin, what is the matter? I thought you were pleased with the idea of staying here. And then, all of a sudden, you—"

He scooped up his garment bag and grabbed for the suitcase. "I'll take the damn attic room." He stalked toward her. She stayed right in his path. He had to halt a foot away from her or knock her down. "Get out of the way."

"No. Really. This is silly. I don't see why you—"

"I won't stay in your damn house, and that's that."

"But I only thought—"

"Don't think. If you want to know where I stand on something, ask me. It's very simple. And much more effective than reading my mind." He took another step. "Move."

She sucked in a small wounded gasp. "You're behaving totally out of proportion about this."

"Move."

She met his gaze, still defiant, for about a count of five. And then, with a tiny defeated sigh, she stepped out of his way. He brushed past her and kept going, headed for the front door.

Chapter Fourteen

Sophie trailed after him as far as the front room. He set down his big suitcase to fling open the door, then grabbed it up again and went through without looking back. Sophie stopped where she was in the middle of the room, watching him leave, wondering how things had gotten so awful so fast. He reached the car, tossed his things in the trunk, shoved the door down, and marched around to the driver's side.

He reached for the doorhandle. And then he stopped. He glanced up at the blue sky and down at the fine shoes on his feet. Finally he turned and looked through the open door of the guest house right at Sophie.

Cautiously she crossed the floor and went out to stand on the porch that ran the width of the house.

Sin started toward her. He stopped at the base of the three steps that led up to where she waited.

"I'm sorry," he said.

She couldn't bring herself to say it was all right; it wasn't. She forced a smile. "I guess we're both a little on edge."

"I meant what I said. I won't put you out of your house."

"Yes. All right."

"Do you still want me to stay?"

She should probably have hesitated, at least. But she didn't. "Yes. I do—and things have slowed down considerably since you were here before. I can put you in a much nicer room." She tried a rueful smile. "I could even see to it that you have your own bath."

He put a foot up on the first step and stuck his hands in his pockets. "A nicer room—with a bath— would be great. But I want it clear that you'll charge me the same as you'd charge anyone."

She hadn't planned to charge him at all. She opened her mouth to protest.

He didn't even let her start. "I swear to you. I can afford to pay for my room."

The black Lexus gleamed in the sun behind him. She looked down at those beautiful shoes of his. "I know you can. I only wanted..." She didn't quite know how to finish.

"What?"

"For you to feel welcome, I guess."

"Do you think you could look at me, instead of my shoes?"

She forced her gaze upward. He wasn't exactly smiling. But then again, he'd never been a big one for smiles. At least he looked reasonably friendly— in that broody, intense way of his.

"I promise to feel welcome," he said, humor lighting his eyes just a little.

She wanted to argue some more, to insist that she didn't feel right about having him pay. But she knew it wouldn't do any good. "All right, then," she conceded. "You'll take a nicer room, complete with its own bath. And I'll charge you for it, full price."

He took his foot off the step and his hands from his pockets. "Come on, then. Better get me checked in."

She gave him the room they called the north suite, so named because its bow window faced that direction, providing a view of the back grounds and the oak grove beyond. She wondered, as she climbed the stairs ahead of him, if he would remember it from his childhood. She was pretty sure it hadn't been his parents' room; the original master suite was in the front of the house. However, the room might hold a few memories for him, anyway.

But Sin said nothing of memories. He dropped his suitcase on the rug, tossed his garment bag over a chair and cast a baleful glance around.

"Where's the phone?"

Patiently she explained that they didn't have much of a phone system. There was a line in the kitchen, which had an extension in Myra's room. And a pay phone in the entrance hall that the guests could use. "It's part of the charm here," she added, sounding sheepish in spite of herself. "The Mountain Star is a place to get away from ringing phones."

He turned those intense black eyes on her. "Which means, in the off-season, you can't count on the executive trade."

"The *executive* trade?" She really did try not to

scoff. "We're not set up for that kind of thing, and we never planned to be. Families come here. And couples looking for a romantic hideaway—"

He dismissed her explanation with a wave of his hand. "Fine. Whatever. I have a cell phone."

"But you could use the kitchen phone. I'm sure that would—"

"No, thanks. I'll manage. I want to get this whole thing moving right away, and that means I'll need a phone to myself."

"To call contractors and get estimates, you mean?"

He gave her another of those dark looks he was such a master at. "That is what I'm here for, isn't it?"

She only stared at him, picturing a phalanx of contractors descending on the Mountain Star, coming up with estimates for extensive improvements she wasn't even sure she wanted made.

He blew out a breath. "All right. What is it?"

"Well, I just don't…"

"What? Speak up."

She squared her shoulders and spoke out loud and clear. "I thought we said we would take it slow."

"We did. I'm getting estimates, that's all. *I* thought that was what we'd agreed I'd do."

It was. And she knew it.

"Sophie, there's no law that says we have to make the improvements right away—or *ever,* for that matter."

"Right."

"We have to start somewhere."

"Of course, we do."

"I want to get an idea of what is possible and what it will cost."

"That does make sense."

He was pacing back and forth. "So what is the problem?"

I love you, and I'm a coward. "Nothing."

He stopped pacing, turned to face her. "Then you're giving me the go-ahead to get the damn estimates?"

"Yes. Certainly. It's what we agreed."

"Well, at least that's settled."

"Yes."

"And once I get all the figures together, we'll sit down with them, all right?"

She nodded.

"We'll see where we want to go from there."

"Yes. That's reasonable. I understand."

"So," Myra said an hour later. "How's our new guest settling in?"

Sophie picked up her fork and started in on the stuffed tomato salad Myra had just set in front of her. She took a bite, chewed and swallowed. "Umm. This is wonderful. What is that spice—cumin?"

"Did I ask you what you thought of lunch? I don't think I asked you that."

Sophie drank some milk and set the glass down carefully. "He seems fine."

"You use that word a lot lately. *Fine.* Have you noticed that?"

"Myra. What are you driving at?"

There was a bowl of fruit on the kitchen table. Myra turned it, moved the bananas from the left side to the right. "I thought you were giving him the guest house."

"He refused to stay there."

"Why?"

"Myra, I don't have the answers to everything."

Myra clucked her tongue. "A little on the prickly side, are we?" She fiddled with the bananas some more. "Maybe you ought to ask him."

"Ask him what?"

"Why he refused the guest house."

Sophie knew her friend was right. "There are a lot of things I ought to ask him."

"And will you?"

Sophie picked up her fork again, then set it down. "I keep meaning to."

"But when *will* you?"

"Soon."

Myra sighed. "Better eat your lunch."

Sophie hardly saw Sin the rest of the day. He spent a couple of hours in his room—no doubt putting his cell phone to use, calling every contractor in the county. And then, later, he went out. He returned in time for dinner and sat down in the dining room with the rest of the guests. Once he'd finished eating, he retreated to his room.

Sophie ate later in the kitchen with Myra and Caleb. Afterward she helped Myra wash dishes and set up for the next morning. Then she crossed the lawn to the guest house. She lay awake very late, thinking of Sin, telling herself to give the situation time—and worrying that he'd never get a moment's sleep over in the cottage, where the past haunted him so terribly.

* * *

In the north suite in Riker cottage, Sin did lay awake. But his sleepless state had nothing to do with being in the cottage.

On that level, he had changed. He wasn't sure exactly how. But as soon as he'd stepped through the front door that morning, he'd realized that no bleak memories would torment him there now.

Perhaps, when he had walked away and left the place to Sophie the month before, he'd let go of more than his obsession to get it back.

In any case, to him Riker cottage was just a big old house now. A structure of wood and rock that needed a new roof and probably ought to have a termite inspection ASAP.

No, the past didn't keep him awake. Sophie did.

Sophie, who might want him and might not. Who had proposed a partnership between them.

Maybe.

Who offered him her bed.

Without her in it.

He had been certain of one thing when he came here this time: that the next move would have to be hers.

But after today, Sin Riker wasn't certain of anything at all.

The next day the contractors started coming. Before noon, Sin had two men crawling on the roof and three going through the kitchen with their tape measures and their clipboards. Since it was Bethy's day off again, Sophie vacuumed and dusted the parlors, foyer, stairs and landings, cleaned the guests' rooms—and tried to stay out of their way.

After lunch, it was more of the same. Sophie made more beds and more contractors appeared. By three, when all of her maid's duties were done, Sin had gone off somewhere. Sophie headed back to the guest house to tackle the accounts.

She'd just settled in at her desk when the phone rang. It was Myra in the main house.

"Jennifer Randall's on her way," Myra said. Jennifer Randall was the owner of Black Angel, the Arabian mare who'd been injured a couple of months before. "She came banging through the back door a minute ago, looking for you."

"She's angry?"

"Steamed."

"Is her horse injured again?"

"Not that she mentioned. She's just on the warpath over something Caleb said, I think."

"Thanks for the warning."

"Good luck."

Sophie hung up just as the pounding started on the back door.

"He is rude. Rude and pushy. And I refuse to board Black Angel here for another day unless you do something about him." Jennifer Randall paced back and forth in front of Sophie's desk.

"Ms. Randall, what exactly did Caleb do?"

"What did he do? What he always does. Treating me as if I don't know how to handle my own horse. Today he actually tried to give me instructions on caring for my tack. I have had it. He is rude. And I don't like his attitude…telling me how to *ride*, for pity's sake. Giving me orders on how to take care of my equipment. I don't have to put up with that. And I won't."

"Ms. Randall, I—"

"Will you do something about him?"

Sophie mentally counted to ten. "Just what is it that you would like me to do?"

"Reprimand him. Make it clear to him that if he wants to keep his job—"

"You're asking me to threaten to fire him?"

The woman froze in midstride and planted both fists on her hips. "Yes. That's exactly what I'm asking."

Patience, Sophie thought. "Ms. Randall, I won't fire Caleb. He does the work of three men around here. All of the others who board horses here consider him an excellent groom. And he's also a dear friend."

"Well. Then I'm afraid I'll have to take Black Angel out of your care."

Sophie opened her mouth to try to dissuade her, and then shut it. She had to face facts here. The boarding fee Jennifer Randall paid every month simply wasn't worth all the trouble she caused.

The woman began pacing again. "Quite frankly, Ms. Jones, this is no way to run a business. Stable help should be just that—help."

"Ms. Randall," Sophie said. "We are sorry to lose Black Angel. But I think you're right. It's for the best."

Jennifer Randall stopped pacing. She turned. "What?"

"Of course you'll need a little time to find another place to board her."

"But I—"

"A few days, is that enough?"

"Why, I—"

Sophie rose. "I'm sorry it hasn't worked out."

The woman sucked in a gasp. "Well, I never—"

"I really don't think there's anything more to say."

"I cannot believe—" This time the woman cut herself off. "All right. I'll make other arrangements. Within the next few days."

"Thank you."

"And I have to tell you, I will *not* be recommending the Mountain Star to any of my friends or associates."

Sophie winced, but made herself say evenly, "I understand."

"And I intended to ride today. I *still* intend to ride today. I expect that man to take good care of Black Angel until I find her a new place."

"Of course. There'll be no problem, I promise you." She delivered those words to Jennifer Randall's back, since the woman had already whirled to flounce out. Sophie sank into her desk chair, wincing again as she heard the kitchen door slam.

Caleb appeared about fifteen minutes later, filling the doorway with his muscular bulk.

Sophie looked up from her computer and gave him a smile. "You okay?"

"I've been better. The Randall woman just rode off on Black Angel. She did come and talk to you, didn't she?"

"She sure did."

"What happened?"

"We agreed that she'd find another stable."

He looked down at the floor. "That's a lot of horse. Someday that woman will get herself thrown bad. Or Black Angel will come up with worse than a sprain."

"Caleb, look at it this way. It's not our problem anymore—or at least it won't be within a few days."

He took a step into the room. "I'm sorry, Sophie B."

"It's not your fault. I know that."

"We can't afford to lose any boarders."

"That one we couldn't afford to keep. Now lighten up. You did the best you could with that woman, and we're lucky we're going to be rid of her."

"I'll always feel bad for poor Black Angel."

"In this situation, there's really nothing you can do."

"I guess I know it."

"Then will you please stop shuffling your feet and acting like the world's come to an end."

He gave her a reasonable semblance of a smile.

She said, "Go on back to the stables. And don't worry. This worked out for the best all the way around."

"I hope you're right."

"I know I am."

As soon as she finished recording the receipts for the previous week and paying a few bills that just couldn't wait another day, Sophie headed for the barn to fool around with her projector some more. The darn thing still wasn't working right.

She saw Sin, out in the driveway saying goodbye to one of his contractors. He waved at her and she almost stopped, to share a few words with him, to see how his day was going. But after yesterday, she hardly knew what to expect from him: another argument, most likely. After dealing with the Randall woman, she just didn't feel up to more conflict right then. She returned his wave and kept on walking.

The contractor got in his pickup and drove away—and seconds later, Sin fell in step with her.

"What's up now?" he asked.

It was an innocent enough question. But still, her stomach clenched like a fist. She just knew he'd find something to criticize soon enough. "I'm going to the barn to look at my projector. It's been acting up."

"Does it ever *not* act up?"

"Good question." She walked a little faster. Next he'd start in on how she needed a new projector.

And he did. "Sophie, we've got to look into replacing that thing."

She murmured something noncommittal and kept on walking.

He stayed with her—and moved on to the next order of business. "What the hell happened to that skinny maid you had?"

"Midge quit a few weeks ago. I have a new maid now. Bethy."

"I didn't see any Bethy today. I saw you cleaning the rooms by yourself."

"Bethy has Monday and Tuesday off." She had no intention of telling him that Bethy was four months pregnant and morning sickness kept her from working most of the rest of the week. He'd find out soon enough, she supposed. And then she'd get an earful on that subject, too.

They had reached the barn. He took one door and she took the other. They swung them wide and braced them open. They entered the cool, dim interior. Sophie pulled open the curtains to the main room and turned on the overhead fluorescents. She spotted an empty plastic bottle down near the screen, so she went to collect it.

Sin remained at the top of the aisle. "What happened with the bossy blonde. The one with the black Arabian mare?"

How could he know about Jennifer Randall? The man must have radar. She scooped up the bottle and started back toward him. "So. You heard about that."

"Pretty hard not to. She came stomping into the kitchen in those tall boots of hers just when I got back from looking over that meadow where we talked about putting my house."

She reached him and went by on her way to the trash can by the concession counter.

He caught her arm. "Stand still a minute, will you?"

She knew that he'd only touched her in order to slow her down. Still, that touch loosed a chain of sensual reactions, like little firecrackers exploding along the waiting surface of her skin. She clutched the empty plastic bottle tighter, hoping the action would help to still her own response.

It didn't.

His face changed, his mouth going softer, his eyes kindling with heat. Those exquisite five nights they'd shared seemed to rise and shimmer in the air between them. She knew he remembered, just as she remembered—the taste of his kisses, the way he used to reach for her, his hand sliding under her hair, cupping her nape, pulling her close....

Abruptly he released her.

"Tell me about the woman," he commanded, all business once more. "The blonde with the black Arabian mare. Some problem with Caleb?"

She blinked. "How did you know?"

"She mentioned the groom when she came storming into the kitchen—and not in a flattering way. How did you work it out?"

"She's taking the horse elsewhere."

"When?"

"I gave her a few days to find another stable."

She waited for him to start criticizing Caleb and mentally braced herself to remain reasonable as she took Caleb's side.

But he surprised her. "Well, the sooner she's out of your hair, the better, the way I see it."

She opened her mouth to argue—and had to switch directions in midword. "I...completely agree with you."

"There's nothing more dangerous than a bad horsewoman who refuses to admit she doesn't know what the hell she's doing."

Unless it's a bad horse*man,* she thought—but decided that since they were agreeing on something, she'd better not push her luck. "Yes. That's true."

"Which reminds me of something else. How well are you insured? Not well enough, I'll bet. We'll have to look into that. Especially since you insist on bedding down the homeless in that *campground* of yours. I went by there today, by the way. You need to get those people to pick up their trash."

She couldn't stop herself from rolling her eyes.

His eyes narrowed. "What does that mean?"

"What?"

"You just rolled your eyes at me."

"I did?"

"You know damn well you did."

"Well..."

"Well, what?"

"Well, Sin, I don't know—"

"Yes, you do."

She drew in a fortifying breath and started again. "I'm feeling a little overwhelmed, that's all. You're so *driven* about all this."

He made a low impatient sound. "There's no sense in fooling around. I have a couple more people coming tomorrow. Then I'll have all the estimates I need. I can tell you what I'm willing to invest here, you can show me your profit-and-loss statements. And we can make our decision."

She felt as if the barn's stone walls had started moving in her. "We can?"

Those black eyes never wavered. "That was the deal, wasn't it?"

"But I thought—"

"What?"

"I thought we'd have more time."

"*I* don't need any more time."

"But..."

"But what?"

"Well, this is all happening so fast. I just don't...I mean, don't you need to get some idea about that house you might build? Don't you need estimates there, too?"

"Sophie. I have plenty of money. I can hire a general contractor—or do the job myself. All that's required is that I make a decision—to do it or not."

She couldn't think of a thing to say to that except, "Oh."

"Sophie."

"Yes?"

"What is going on here?"

She backed up a step.

"I know this is probably a shock, coming from me, but I think it's time we got honest with each other."

"Honest?" She repeated the word as if unsure of its meaning.

He raised a sardonic brow. "Yes. Honest. As in you tell me your truth and I'll tell you mine."

She thought suddenly of little Anthea Jones, bobbing down the river in her orange life jacket—out of her depth and out of control. "I don't...what truth?"

He ran a hand back through his hair. "Look. I think you're going to have to decide just what the hell you want from me."

She retreated another step. "I...we...I mean..."

"Do you even *know* what you want from me?"

Her hands felt all sweaty and her throat felt so tight. "I..."

He didn't relent. "I asked you a question. Do you know what you want from me?"

She almost moved back a third step—and then somehow managed to hold her ground. "Yes. I do. I know."

"What?"

"I..."

"Say it."

And somehow she did. "I want you to come back to me. I want us to be together. The way we were before."

Oh, dear Lord, she had done it! She had gotten the words out at last....

Unfortunately Sin didn't seem very impressed. "This isn't before."

How could a man be so obtuse? "Well, I know that."

"Are you sure?"

"Well. Certainly. Yes. Of course, I'm sure."

"Listen to you." His voice was gentle, forgiving. Kind. She hated that. She was the gentle one, the kind one. Not him. "You don't sound sure. And you don't behave as if you're sure. Not by a long shot."

"I…" How could she tell him? Why did he refuse to understand? "I…came to LA. To find you. I was hoping…"

"Hoping what?"

"That we could work things out."

"You offered me a partnership, Sophie. A business agreement."

She experienced an utterly childish urge to hurl the plastic bottle at him. "Because I didn't know how…to reach out to you. I didn't know what else to do."

"So, you never really wanted a partnership at all?"

"I…" Not another word came into her mind.

He kept pushing. "*I,* what?"

She could have cried. Just sat down on the plank floor and sobbed her heart out. "Oh, Sin, I…"

"*What?*"

She confessed in a small voice, "I guess I just want you."

"You *guess?*"

Oh, this was not going the way she'd imagined at all. She'd *told* him that she wanted him. Didn't that count for anything at all?

Apparently not. "All right," he said grimly. "You want me. You *guess* you want me."

Anger, frustration, longing—they were all tangled up inside her. "I *do.*" She forced some conviction into her voice. "I do want you."

"You want me. The way it was before."

"Yes." She clutched the empty bottle hard again. "And I have to know. Do you want me?"

He was shaking his head.

She wanted to scream, stomp her foot, tear her hair. "What does that mean, shaking your head like that? Does it mean you don't want me, after all?"

He made a low noise in his throat. "I don't think that's the question."

"It is too the question!" She only realized she was shouting when the pigeon up in the rafters took flight in distress. Sophie let out a startled cry as the bird came at them, swooping past Sin and down on Sophie. She ducked. It flew on by, through the pulled-back curtains, and out the wide-open doors. Sophie stared after it, thinking of all the times she'd tried to chase it away. And now, just like that, the bird was gone.

"Sophie."

She had no choice but to face him.

"Come here."

She froze, riddled with suspicion. Torn in two with yearning. So confused. Nothing made sense anymore. Nothing at all. "Why?"

"Just come here."

She didn't want to go to him—and at the same time, she wanted nothing else.

She took one awful step forward. And then another. And then the one that brought her right up close to him.

"I'm here, aren't I?" he asked quietly. "Why the hell would I come here if I didn't want you?"

She had no answer for that. She had no answer for anything.

He raised a hand. She flinched.

He made a soothing sound. And then he traced the line of her hair where it fell along her cheek, a caress that sent heated shivers singing all through her. His hand moved down, over the curve of her jaw to her neck. It paused at the place where her pulse beat so fast—and then continued on to the little hollow at the base of her throat. He stroked that hollow lightly, gently. The tangle of emotions inside her shifted, resolving themselves into one dominant sensation: desire.

"I can't seem to forget the feel of you." Low and caressing, his voice curled around her. "It's kept me awake a lot of nights...."

All she could whisper was, "Yes..."

"You remember, too."

Again she murmured, "Yes."

He turned his hand over, brushed the side of her throat with the back of his index finger. "Those five nights we had together, do you want them again?"

She licked her lips and nodded.

He raised his other hand, cupped her face. And brought his mouth down on hers.

Chapter Fifteen

Sophie dropped the plastic bottle. She heard it roll quietly away.

And then she forgot all about it.

Sin's mouth moved on hers, at first coaxing—then demanding her response.

She opened for him, sighing. His tongue mated with hers as he wrapped his arms around her and pulled her close against him.

He was hard. She moaned at the feel of him.

And then he put his hands on her shoulders. His fingers dug in, hurting her a little. He put her away from him.

"I'd say that answers your question." He dropped his arms, backed away another step.

All she wanted was his lips on hers. She swayed toward him. "Sin—"

He took her shoulders once more, steadying her. "Let's just get this whole thing clear."

"I don't—"

"You want me. I want you. I don't see *wanting* as the issue at all. Do you, *honestly?*"

Her body thrummed with yearning. Why wouldn't he simply sweep her into his arms again?

"Sophie. Answer me."

She shrugged off his hands, ordered her traitorous body to stop making a fool of her. "Yes. I mean, no. All right. We...want each other."

"Exactly. And we can be lovers, the way we were before. At least, for a while." His fine mouth twisted in a wry grin. "However, in my experience, that kind of thing never lasts all that long."

"But I—"

"You *did* say that you wanted it to be the way it was before."

Oh, why did he refuse to understand? "I meant that we were so close. We never argued. We were... intimate, in the best kind of way."

"Sophie. It was all based on lies. Is that what you want?"

"Of course not. You're twisting what I've said."

"No, I'm making a point."

"What point?"

"That partnership you offered, that was a good idea."

What in heaven's name was he getting at now? "It was?"

He nodded. "If we're going to be together, we're going to have to share. And I think that's our problem."

He was making no sense at all. "Sharing? *Sharing* is our problem?"

"Yes. Neither of us has a clue how to do it."

She could not get her mind around the utter unfairness of that statement. She shared all she had. She helped others daily. And he knew it. Wasn't he always complaining about her campground? And what about the Mountain Star itself, forever on the verge of going under because she was such a sucker for someone in need?

She told him quite proudly, "I know how to share."

He was shaking his head again. "Uh-uh. You know how to *give*. The two are not the same." He smiled then. A real, rueful, tender sort of smile. "I think you like what you have here, and you're not sure you want to share. And I do understand that. I felt the same way. Once upon a time."

A thousand arguments scrolled through her head at once, but not one of them found its way out her mouth.

He had more to say. "Do you want a lover, Sophie? Is that all you want from me? I would be that for you. For a while. As a matter of fact, I'm kind of at loose ends now. Considering a career change, considering a *lot* of changes. I wouldn't mind a little...diversion. Something to pass the time while I figure out what to do with the rest of my life."

"A...diversion?"

He lifted one shoulder in an elegant shrug. "Why not? I find you extremely...diverting." His gaze traveled over her, searing where it touched. "Is that what you're really after here? Just a little diversion?"

"I...no, of course not."

"Well, then, I'll get my estimates together. By to-morrow evening, how's that?"

She swallowed and somehow managed a reply. "All right."

Without another word, he brushed past her. She turned and watched him vanish the same way the bird had gone—through the curtains and out the doors.

That night, Sin didn't appear for dinner at six-thirty with the rest of the guests. Instead, he showed up in the kitchen an hour later, just as Myra and Sophie were about to sit down.

"I wonder, Myra—have you got an extra plate for me?"

Myra folded her freckled arms and gave him a slow once-over. "I imagine I could dig one up."

"I would appreciate it."

Myra got down another plate, a set of flatware and a fresh napkin. She set him a place.

"Thank you," he said.

The cook cast a fretful glance toward Caleb's empty chair. "Now, where is Caleb?"

"He'll be in," said Sophie, picking up her napkin, trying not to let her gaze collide with Sin's. Since he'd left her in the barn that afternoon, she hadn't been able to stop thinking of the hungry way he'd kissed her—not to mention the hard things he'd said. The more she dwelled on his words, the more disturbing truth she found in them.

She *didn't* want to share the Mountain Star. It was hers, she had created it to be just what it was. And she feared that Sin wanted to make it into something else altogether.

She shuddered every time she thought of what it

might become, with phones and fax machines in every room and busy, impatient executive types running in and out. Everything new and shining and…antiseptic. A place where neither her campground nor her theater would really fit in. She didn't want that. Not on her life.

But, oh, she did want Sin. And she knew that to have him more than temporarily, some kind of compromise would have to be reached.

Tomorrow night.

Too soon.

Much too soon.

"Sophie B.," Myra said.

"Um, yes?"

"Mr. Riker just asked you to pass the rice."

"Oh. Yes. Of course." She picked up the bowl and tried not to look directly at him as she handed it to him.

"Thank you."

"You're welcome."

Sophie heard the back door open. That would be Caleb. She steeled herself for the surly attitude he'd assume as soon as he saw who had joined them for dinner.

But Caleb hardly glanced at Sin. He came and stood by his chair, where he shifted from foot to foot the way he always did when something upset him.

"Sit down," commanded Myra. "Eat."

Caleb spoke to Sophie. "That Randall woman never did come back today. And I'm gettin' real worried. It'll be dark soon."

Sophie set down her fork. "Do you know which way she went?"

Caleb nodded. ''That trail that heads northeast, up into the mountains.''

Sophie tucked her napkin beside her plate and stood. ''Come on, then. We'd better go and find her.''

Sin's chair scraped the floor. ''I'm going, too.''

Caleb grunted and cast Sin a dismissing look. ''We can handle this ourselves.''

Sin swore. ''Look. That woman has gone and gotten herself lost on my land. There's no way I'm staying behind.''

By ten of eight, with perhaps a half an hour of daylight left, Sin, Sophie and Caleb were mounted, armed with electric lanterns and on their way.

The wind had come up. It blew at their backs as they headed out. Caleb led them on the path he'd seen the woman take, around east of the cottage, and then to the north across the meadow of wild roses.

Once beyond the meadow, they started climbing up into the mountains. The face of the full moon grew brighter above them as the sun sank behind the western hills. The wind blew harder, making the trees rustle and sway.

It was full dark when they found Black Angel, peacefully nibbling grass in a clear spot between two huge, old cedar trees, her ebony mane swirling. Caleb dismounted and approached her. She looked up, whinnied in recognition, and came right to him.

He patted her neck and murmured in her ear. Then he turned to Sin and Sophie. ''The rein's broken, leather sawed clean through.'' He shook his head. ''I warned that damn woman....''

A really strong gust of wind blew by them, stirring the horses, making them dance. Sin looked up at the moon. "We can't search much longer. It's getting too late. We should bring the sheriff in on this."

Caleb suggested, "It'll be another hour before they can get their people mobilized. Let's go on a little ways."

Sin frowned. "But not far."

"All right."

They hobbled Black Angel so she wouldn't wander off and rode on through the trees that seemed to close in around them, blocking out the pale glow of the moon. Soon enough, they had to switch on the big lantern flashlights to see the trail ahead.

Caleb spotted the little riding hat, blown against a tree trunk, about a half mile from where they'd come upon Black Angel. The groom swung down from the spotted gelding he rode and grabbed it up. "It's hers." The three shared a look.

Sin made the decision. "Let's go on."

Caleb remounted. The wind shoved at them, blowing hard, strong now even in the shelter of the trees. At last they reached a rocky stretch. The trees thinned out to nothing—and Jennifer Randall came limping at them, falling, picking herself up, staggering forward, and sobbing as she tried to run.

"Oh, thank God! Help. You have to help...." She stumbled down on them, her hands out, her face smudged and her hair wild in the whipping wind. The horses grew nervous, they pranced and tried to shy away from her, dislodging rocks that tumbled down the mountain behind them.

Sin passed his lantern to Sophie and swung out of the saddle. The Randall woman fell into his arms—and then immediately started struggling to get free. "Oh, God. Oh, we have to hurry...."

Sin tried to calm her. "Hold on. Slow down…"

"No. Listen. I…had to start a fire. I was hoping someone would see and come rescue me. But then the wind…oh, we have to hurry! We have to hurry now!"

They all understood then what the woman meant.

"Douse the lanterns," Sin commanded.

Sophie and Caleb obeyed. The world went dark. They looked higher up the mountain. There, rising above the thick crown of trees, ribbons of smoke spiraled in an eerie, curling dance toward the silvery moon.

"Come on." Sin put an arm around the Randall woman. "We've got to move." He helped her over to the others, stopping beside Caleb's horse.

The woman's handsome face turned ugly beneath its layer of grime. "No. I will not ride with that—"

Sin spun her to face him. "We don't have time for any of your games now."

The woman looked into those hard, dark eyes, bit her lip—and nodded.

Caleb put a hand down and Sin hoisted her up in front of the groom. Then he went to his own horse, lifted the flap on the saddlebag, and brought out his cell phone. The wind whistled hard around them as Sin punched up 911.

They had some degree of luck. The wind didn't turn. They found Black Angel where they'd left her and led her back with them.

They were crossing the meadow where the wild roses grew when the first helicopter sailed by overhead, laden with fire retardant to drop on the blaze.

"Most beautiful sight I ever saw," Caleb declared,

watching as the copter swung away toward the mountains behind them.

"Let's just pray they're in time to contain the damn thing," Sin added bleakly.

Jennifer Randall whined, "Can we please get moving? I need a doctor. My ankle is killing me."

At the Mountain Star, the firefighters in their cross-country vehicles were already arriving. The head of the team took a few precious minutes to question the Randall woman, then suggested someone drive her to Sierra Nevada Memorial to have her ankle x-rayed. Myra volunteered for that job. Sophie cast the cook a grateful glance.

As the owner of the property, Sin was allowed to head back out with the firefighters. He suggested they also take Caleb along, to show them the smoothest way overland.

Sophie stepped up. "I'd like to go, too."

Sin focused those eyes on her. "Stay here. You have guests to worry about."

His imperious tone rankled. And she feared she might go crazy, sitting there, doing nothing, just waiting for news. But she knew he was right.

In the cottage, the guests gravitated toward the kitchen, where Sophie kept Myra's radio tuned to a local station, which provided periodic reports on the fire. They all clustered around the big table, sharing pot after pot of Myra's coffee, telling old stories of other forest fires they'd heard about or seen, falling silent whenever the radio announcer came on with more news. Overhead, through the hours, they heard the helicopters rattling by.

Myra returned at a little after ten to report that Jennifer Randall had no broken bones. "A bad sprain is all."

"Where is she now?" Sophie asked.

"I drove her home. She complained all the way—that her ankle hurt and her nerves were shot. She says she's going to sell that horse of hers. You should have heard her." Myra stuck her nose in the air and pursed her mouth. "'Black Angel has become totally unmanageable.' That's exactly what she said."

One of the guests asked, "You're talking about the woman who started the fire?"

"I'm afraid so," Sophie said.

The guest shook his head. "If the forest service had any sense, they'd stick her with the bill for this mess."

A murmur of agreement went up from the others.

Sophie stood. "How about more coffee?"

"I'll have some."

"Me, too."

Myra clucked her tongue. "I'll get it." She bustled over to the counter to get the pot.

By midnight, the wind had died down. The radio announcer said the fire was ninety-five percent contained. There would be no more reports unless it kicked up again. They heard the firefighters returning, driving past the house and out to the highway. No more beating helicopter blades disturbed the quiet of the mountain night.

The guests wandered back to their rooms, keyed up from too much coffee, but all determined to try to get some sleep. Caleb came in at twelve-thirty, to find Sophie and Myra in the kitchen alone.

"It's gonna be okay," he said. "They got to it soon enough. It looks like Sin's lost about ten acres of trees. But he said he could afford that just fine."

"*Sin?*" Sophie asked gently.

Caleb shuffled his feet. "All right. He's not so bad. I could get used to him if I had to—just as long as he doesn't go breaking your heart again."

Myra demanded, "But where is he now?"

"He's comin'. He waited to ride back on the last truck. Should be here pretty soon now."

The cook pushed her bulk out of her chair. "Caleb, you didn't eat a bite of dinner. Let me—"

"Naw. I'm not hungry. I want to check on the horses and get me a little sleep." Caleb headed out the back door, leaving Sophie and Myra alone again. Sophie turned to her friend—and found those green eyes studying her.

"You'll be waiting up for him, won't you?"

They both knew who Myra meant by "him." In lieu of an answer, Sophie picked up an empty coffee cup and carried it to the sink.

"Do you love that man?" Myra said to her back.

Sophie set the cup down and turned to face her friend.

Myra asked again more gently, "Well, do you?"

Sophie told the truth. "Yes."

"Does he love you?"

"He's never said."

"Maybe you should ask him."

"Maybe." Sophie looked down at the floor, then up at Myra once again. "If he and I...worked things out, there would be some changes around here."

Myra pushed in her chair. "No sense in running from change. It always finds a person anyway."

* * *

Once Myra headed up the back stairs, Sophie sat at the table alone, waiting and listening for the sound of that last truck coming in. Eventually she got up, washed out the coffeepot and set it up for the next morning. There were a few dishes waiting in the sink. She opened the dishwasher and loaded them in.

At ten after one, she heard the sound of a vehicle outside. She froze in the act of wiping a counter. The sound faded away quickly toward the front of the cottage. Sophie still didn't move. She strained to hear the front door opening, but that sound never came.

She looked down at the sponge she'd been using to wipe up counters that were already clean—and realized that if she wanted to speak with Sin, she would have to go looking for him.

She dropped the sponge and ran out through the west parlor to the front hall, where she threw back the old door and hurried out onto the walk. She caught a glimpse of taillights disappearing toward the highway.

And that was all. The moon shone on the grass, making it gleam whitely. Somewhere off in the trees, a dove cooed. The crickets played their never-ending, chirruping song. And off to her left, the little-girl statue still laughed without sound as the water from the fountain cascaded down.

She ventured farther along the walk, out under the broad pale face of the moon. The night was still, the wind that had threatened such havoc faded away now to nothing but a hint of a breeze. On that breeze she could faintly smell wood smoke, an acrid reminder of disaster averted.

Wood smoke. Crickets. The splash of water in the fountain and the gentle cooing of a dove. But no sign of the man she'd been waiting for.

Still, Sophie knew where to find him.

Chapter Sixteen

He sat on the black rock, his back to her, looking out over the dark creek that flowed by a few feet away.

Sophie tiptoed across the soft bed of moss, coming up on his left side, and then hovering there, not sure how to begin.

He turned his head and his eyes met hers. He didn't look surprised to see her.

She asked too brightly, "Is there room for me on that rock?"

He said nothing—but he did scoot a little to the right, leaving a space for her beside him. Carefully she edged onto the rock and sat down.

"Clouds gathering," he said.

She followed his gaze. A grayness crept across the sky, blotting out the stars and drifting in gauzy tendrils over the broad face of the moon.

She said, "Rain would be good to finish off whatever's left of the fire."

He looked at her again. "We were lucky. This time."

She dipped her head in a brief nod. "I know."

"The land needs tending, Sophie. Whatever happens between you and me, I'm going to take steps to thin out some of those trees."

"I understand."

He stared at her for several seconds, his eyes hard, as if he didn't believe she understood at all. Then he turned his gaze to the dark waters of the creek once again.

She waited, not sure how to talk to him, doubting that he even wanted her there. The creek murmured softly as it flowed by and the leaves of the willows and oaks rustled, whispering to each other in the now-gentle wind.

Finally she drummed up enough nerve to reach out and lay her hand on his arm. The contact, as always, sent desire singing through her. She concentrated on ignoring it, on finding the right words to say. "Sin, I can't tell you how much I appreciate the way you dealt with Jennifer Randall tonight. In fact, if you hadn't been here—"

His hand closed over hers. "Don't."

"But I—"

"Don't thank me. No damn testimonials. Not now. Not tonight."

She swallowed, nodded. "All right."

Slowly he brought her hand to his mouth. His lips brushed her fingertips. She hitched in a gasp and he smiled, black eyes gleaming, both feral and knowing at once. "If you're so grateful, then show me."

She closed her own eyes, drew in a breath and let it out slowly. "How?"

His teeth scraped the pads of her fingers, so lightly. "You know."

And she did. She knew very well.

He pushed his other hand beneath her hair and clasped her nape, just the way he used to do. She shuddered in longing. The scent of him teased her: sweat—and wood smoke, from the now-vanquished fire.

"Kiss me." It was a command.

It never entered her mind to disobey. She lifted her mouth and he took it fiercely, holding her head still as he plundered the secrets beyond her lips. She felt his teeth, rasping, scraping the inner surface of her lower lip.

She had no choice but to kiss him back—and not because he demanded it, but because she hungered as he did. Because her whole body yearned.

With a lost cry, she reached for him, clutching his strong shoulders, the need in her rising, answering his. Her tongue met his, twining. She pressed herself against him, offering her body, reckless, on fire....

Then, without warning, he tore his mouth away from her.

Oh, how could he do that? She couldn't bear for it to end. Her need for him seemed to hang there, pulsing like a heart, in the charged air between them.

With another pleading cry, she tried to hold the kiss.

But he kept that from happening, his hands gripping her shoulders. He whispered roughly against her parted lips, "This damn rock's too hard."

She stared at his mouth, dazed, longing for his kiss

again—and yet knowing that making love right now would fix nothing, really. Too much remained unresolved between them. Too much begged to be said.

He frowned at her. "Don't even start."

She blinked. "What?"

"Thinking."

"But, Sin—"

He rolled off his side of the rock and reached for her hand. "Come on."

"I don't... Where?"

"To that guest house of yours."

They went in through the back door. He led her to the front room from there. And then he left her in the middle of the floor and dropped into one of her two overstuffed chairs.

His dark gaze ran over her. "Take off that shirt."

She looked down at the front of herself and then back up at him.

"Take it off."

So she did, unbuttoning each button very carefully, her fingers awkward and slow. Finally she had all the buttons undone. She slipped it over her shoulders.

"Let it drop."

The shirt whispered to the floor.

"Now the bra."

She reached behind her, undid the clasp. Holding the scrap of lace against her breasts to keep it from falling, she slid the straps down.

"Sophie. Let it go."

She straightened her arms. The bra dropped away.

He rose from the chair and approached her, taking her hand, leading her to the sofa. "Lie down."

She obeyed. He knelt at her feet, pulled off her

boots and her socks. Then his hands found the snap of her jeans, flicked it open, took the zipper down. She stared into his eyes as he peeled the jeans off, taking her underpants with them.

At last, she lay naked to his gaze.

He began to caress her, teasing, arousing—laying claim to every inch of her.

He parted her thighs. His dark head dipped between them. Sensation rolled over her, a wave of fire, consuming as it took her down.

"It's raining," he whispered, his hand at the heart of her again.

She listened to the soft pattering on the roof as her body lifted, opened, invited him once again. She moaned, and the rain went on, soft and insistent as her own hungry sighs.

They went to the bedroom. She helped him undress, her hands working swiftly now, undoing all the buttons, pushing the shirt back and off his hard shoulders.

She wrapped her arms around him, felt the teasing scrape of chest hair against her aching breasts. And then she was sliding down to her knees, parting the fly of those black jeans he wore, eagerly taking him into her mouth.

Sometime later, they lay across the bed.

His lips closed over her breast, drawing deep, pulling the need from inside her once again. He let go, looked into her eyes. "Do you still hear the rain?"

She nodded, her fingers combing through his silky hair, listening to the soft, insistent drumming sound.

His hand strayed down, found her—tender, wet, open. Brazenly ready for him.

He arched a dark brow. "This doesn't solve anything, does it?"

She bit her lip, shook her head—and then cried out as his fingers delved in.

He reached across her, opened the drawer in the nightstand, brought out the small box. With great care, he peeled open the foil wrapper. "Help me."

They lay on their sides, facing each other. He wrapped her leg over his hip. She hitched in a breath as he filled her.

He put his hand on her nape again, held her eyes with his own—and began to move.

When the fulfillment came that time, the words rose inside her, pushing so hard, needing to get out.

She started to say them. "I lov—"

He put his hand on her mouth. "No. Don't. Not tonight...."

"But I—"

"No."

She moaned. The words retreated. All that remained was the two of them, the sweet hot point of connection.

The end came, swift and complete, shuddering outward from the center of her, blotting out everything, even the rain.

Chapter Seventeen

Sin woke right at dawn. He opened his eyes and saw Sophie asleep beside him, the covers pulled close around her against the morning chill.

He wanted to reach for her.

But he didn't.

He shouldn't have seduced her last night. She was already confused when it came to him. What had happened last night would only serve to confuse her further.

He slid to the side and lowered his feet to the floor, careful to disturb the covers as little as possible. Once free of the bed, he gathered up his strewn clothing and crept out to the kitchen. A few minutes later he slipped outside fully dressed.

He tried the back door of the cottage. It was open. Inside, the smells of breakfast greeted him: bacon, coffee, biscuits. Myra stood at the counter by the sink, peeling the rind off half a cantaloupe.

He had a thoroughly sleazy urge to try and slink past her.

Before he could decide whether to act on that urge, she turned and spotted him. "I suppose I don't have to wonder where *you've* been." She held the half cantaloupe in one hand and brandished a paring knife with the other.

He knew that anything he said at that point would only make things worse. So he gave her a shrug.

She made a sort of *tsking* sound and waved that knife again. "Are you going to marry that girl or not?"

He shrugged again. "I doubt if she'll have me."

Myra looked at the knife and then at him. She grunted. "All right. Go on with you. Have a hot shower. It looks like you need one."

He turned and made for the stairs.

After his shower, he shaved. He put on clean clothes. By then, twenty minutes had passed since he'd mounted the stairs. He knew he'd lose his mind if he stayed in that room. So he yanked open the door and got out.

Myra was watching for him, standing at the stove this time. "Are you eating with us, then?"

"I'm not hungry." He started for the back door.

She slid her bulk sideways, just enough to block his path. "A man needs a good breakfast."

He gave her his hardest, meanest glare—the one that had never failed to send everyone at Inkerris, Incorporated, scurrying for cover.

Myra grunted and waved a freckled hand. "Fine. Be that way." Grunting a second time, she stepped aside. He brushed past her. She called to his back as he went out the door, "You'll never know unless you ask her!"

Outside, the air was brisk and cool, everything smelling wet and fresh from last night's rain. He started walking fast. He didn't realize he was headed for the stables until he got there.

He found Caleb brushing the black Arabian mare. The groom turned and saw him, brush pausing in mid-stroke.

"One damn fine horse," Sin said, for lack of any better remark.

Caleb left the stall and latched it behind him. "Breakfast time."

"That's what Myra said."

"You coming?"

"I'm not hungry, thanks."

Caleb shook his head. "Not goin' so good, huh— with Sophie B.?"

Sin felt no desire at all to answer that one, so he kept his mouth shut.

Caleb added, "I'll send her on out here as soon as I see her." He tossed the brush.

Sin caught it. "Just because you send her doesn't mean she'll come."

The groom grinned at that. "She is a bossy one, under all that sweetness. She likes running things."

"I noticed."

"But she could be convinced to change a little. By a good man."

Sin felt a rueful smile lift the corners of his mouth. "A *good* man?"

Caleb nodded. "Some men aren't as much as they think they are. And some men are more."

"You think so?"

"I know so. I seen it for myself."

"Sin?"

No answer.

Sophie sat up, pushed back the covers and swung her feet to the floor. Outside the lace-curtained window opposite the bed, the sky was an innocent blue, the clouds all cleared away. Drops of water from the rain still clung to a rosebush that grew thick and thorny, tied to a short trellis just beyond the glass. Heavy dew silvered the lawn.

"Sin?"

Only silence.

He must have left—without waking her, without a word. She hung her head, stared down at her bare knees. They had goose bumps all over them. The room was *cold*.

She jumped up and ran to the bureau to find some clothes, pausing to glance at the clock by the bed before she put them on. It wasn't that late. Myra would be putting breakfast on the table about now.

Oh, where had Sin gone?

And why had he left her to wake up alone?

She remembered the night before, her knees going weak at the sheer erotic beauty of it. But then her need to find Sin snapped some strength into them.

She pulled on clean underwear and padded to the bathroom, where she rinsed her face and tugged a comb through her tangled hair. Then she yanked on the rest of her clothes and headed for the cottage.

She found Myra and Caleb in the kitchen, about to sit down to breakfast.

Myra was setting the plates around. She glanced up

and clucked her tongue disapprovingly. "There you are. Bethy just called. She says she's feeling pretty queasy and won't be able to come in today."

Sophie closed her eyes, rubbed her temples. "I'll have to talk to her."

"You'll have to *fire* her, and you know it."

"We'll see—listen, have you seen Sin this morning?"

Myra and Caleb shared a look. Then Myra confessed, "He came in a half an hour ago, then went out again. Without his breakfast." The words were informational, but the tone was pure mother hen. "I guess we all know where that man was all night."

Sophie blew out a breath. "Myra..."

"When are you going to settle this mess with him?"

"Just tell me. Where is he now?"

Caleb spoke up then. "He's in the stables. I left him there a few minutes ago."

She found him standing at Black Angel's stall, just looking at the horse, who wasn't paying any attention at all to him.

At the sound of Sophie's footsteps, he turned. He held a brush in his hand.

She made herself ask, though it came out all ragged-sounding, "Why...did you just leave?"

He tossed the brush onto a low stool near the rough plank wall.

"Sophie..." His voice sounded as torn as her own.

They stared at each other.

And at that moment, she knew.

He loved her, too. As much as she had ever loved him.

And probably more.

"Oh, Sin…"

He forked a hand through his hair. "I shouldn't have done that last night. I shouldn't have—"

She couldn't bear the distance between them and hurried to close it, stopping just inches away. "Don't apologize. Please."

He closed his eyes. "I can't take this. I hate this."

She reached out, put her hand on his arm. "I know…"

He looked down at where she touched him, then into her eyes once again. "You don't know. You can't know. I…don't know what I'm doing anymore. Since I met you, I don't know who the hell I am."

She clutched his arm harder. "It's all right."

He laughed then, a painful sound. "You said that the first night. Remember? When I grabbed you on the back stairs of the cottage?"

"I remember."

"And you were wrong. It wasn't all right. It was all a damn lie."

"We got past the lies."

He pulled away, stepped back. "You don't trust me anymore—not that I blame you."

She couldn't let him think that—even if it was just a little bit true. "But I do. I do trust you now."

"You don't. And I *want* you to trust me. Which is insane. I've never been the kind of man who gave a damn for a woman's trust."

She tried to make him see her side. "I just…we're so different. In what we want for this place. And I'm afraid. You're so strong. So…determined. You could make the Mountain Star successful, but then it might not really be the Mountain Star anymore."

He said it again, so sadly, "You don't trust me."

And right then, they both heard the low sound.

Sin's eye's hardened. "What's that?"

Sophie glanced down the stalls, to where she thought the sound had come from. "I don't know."

The sound came again—a groan. Someone groaning.

Sin spun on his heel and strode down the rows of stalls. Sophie followed after him.

At the last stall, one that looked empty, he stopped. "In here." He swung open the gate.

Bearded, filthy, dressed in tattered jeans and a grimy sweatshirt, a man huddled, shuddering, against the far wall.

Chapter Eighteen

At the sight of Sin and Sophie, the fellow cried out, put his filthy hands over his face and backpedaled madly. It was as if he thought he could push his starved body through the wall—and away from the two who had found his hiding place. "No, no, don't! I'll go...I'll get out...."

Sophie moved toward him. Sin caught her arm. "Let me."

She felt a powerful urge to shake him off and rush around him. But she made herself curb it. She nodded. "All right."

Sin took one cautious step, and then another. The man drew tighter and tighter against the rough wall. Convulsive shivers rattled through him and his eyes gleamed feverishly bright. "I...went to the camp-ground. I heard it was all right, that a man could bed down there, find peace for a night. But the rain came. It got cold...."

Sin reached him, knelt beside him, spoke with aching gentleness. "You needed a dry place."

"Yeah. A dry place..." The thin body shook harder.

"It's okay," Sin whispered. "It's all right...." He reached in his pocket, came out with a key and tossed it to Sophie. She reacted just fast enough to snare it from the air. "Get the Lexus," he commanded. "We'll take him to the hospital."

"No!" A bony hand shot out, closed over Sin's arm. "I can't afford no hospital."

"It's all right," Sin answered softly. "I can."

The fevered eyes shone brighter—with stubborn pride. "Don't want no charity."

"Don't worry," Sin reassured him. "We don't offer charity here. We have what you need. And there'll be work to do later in exchange."

The man squinted, peered closer at Sin. "Who are you, anyway?"

"Call me Sin."

A ragged laugh escaped the man then, a laugh that turned to a racking cough. When the cough finally subsided, he muttered with some humor, "Sin, eh? I guess I know you already."

"I'm sure you do. What can I call you?"

"Jake. The name's Jake."

"Come on, Jake. Let's get you to a doctor." Sin cast a glance over his shoulder. Sophie hadn't moved.

She *couldn't* move. She could only stare at Sin, thinking of how she had loved him, right from that first night. Of how he had lied to her, how he had taken her innocence, abused her trust.

And how it didn't matter anymore. Because in the end, he had become everything she'd ever dreamed of in a man.

"The car?" Sin demanded.

She shook herself. "Yes. Right away." She turned and ran, out the east door of the stable and across the front driveway to the long garage that branched off the side of the cottage.

Sophie drove to the hospital. Sin sat in the back with Jake. When they arrived, Sin filled out all the forms, taking responsibility for the cost of the sick man's care.

"It's acute pneumonia," the doctor said an hour later. "We've pumped him full of antibiotics and we're getting fluids into him. Now, we'll just have to wait and see."

At a little before eleven, Sin and Sophie got back in the Lexus and returned to the Mountain Star. It was a silent ride. At the cottage, Myra was waiting for them.

"Where on God's earth have you been?"

Sin explained briefly about Jake.

Myra shook her head in sympathy for the poor fellow, then insisted they sit down and have a bite to eat. "And after that, Sophie B., you'd better get going on those rooms."

Sin stopped in the act of pouring himself a cup of coffee. "I thought you said you'd hired someone to replace that maid who quit."

"Sure she did," Myra scoffed. "Bethy's her name. She's got a baby on the way and she's always calling in sick."

Sophie sank to the table. "I realize I have to talk with her." She waited for Sin to start in on her.

But he only carried the cup he'd filled over to the table and set it down before her. "Have some coffee."

She looked up at him in sheer gratitude—for what he hadn't said. "Thank you."

"And you," Myra said sternly.

Sin glanced her way. "Me?"

"Yes, you. Some man called about insulation. He's coming at two."

As soon as she'd eaten, Sophie got right to work cleaning rooms. At one, Myra called her down to the kitchen and gestured at the phone. "It's Bethy."

Sophie picked it up reluctantly—only to learn that Bethy had decided to move to Fresno, where she could live with another sister and work in a florist's shop.

"I'm so sorry to let you down like this," Bethy said, sounding much more contrite than she ever had all the times she'd called in sick.

Sophie smiled at the phone in pure relief and promised Bethy that she'd manage somehow.

Myra was frowning as Sophie hung up. "What now?"

"Bethy's moving to Fresno to work in her other sister's flower shop."

One of Myra's red eyebrows inched toward her hairline. "That means we have a chance to hire someone who'll actually do the job."

"Exactly."

"No sad cases this time," Myra bargained. "Promise me. Someone who'll show up on time and stay till the work's done."

Sophie raised her right hand, palm out. "I do solemnly swear."

Myra harrumphed. "I'll believe it when I see it."

Sophie finished the rooms at a little after two. By then, Sin was busy with the insulation specialist. Sophie wandered downstairs and out the back door. She waved at Caleb, who was riding the old tractor mower across the broad lawn.

At the guest house, she showered and changed into one of her favorite dresses—the one she'd been wearing the first night she met Sin. She went back outside next and chose three red roses from the bush just beyond her bedroom window. She carried them back to the cottage, found a small crystal vase in the cupboard, and took the bouquet up the back stairs to Sin's room.

It looked lovely on the small stand by the bed. Sophie set it down and turned it, so the velvety red blooms were facing out.

"My mother loved roses." His voice came from the doorway behind her.

She turned to him, a smile trembling across her mouth. "I hope you do, too."

He didn't even glance at them. His eyes were all for her. "They're beautiful. Thank you." Then he stepped beyond the threshold and closed the door. That brooding gaze took a slow tour of her, from her head to her toes.

He said, "Your slip is showing."

She smoothed her skirt, drew her shoulders back. "It's not a slip."

"I know. It's a *petticoat*."

She felt as if she might cry. "You...remember."

"I do."

Turning away just a little, she swiped at her eyes. "Is the insulation man gone?"

He closed the distance between them, guided her chin around. "He's gone."

She moved in a fraction closer, lifted her mouth. "Will you...kiss me, please?"

Light as a rose petal, his lips brushed over hers. "You were wonderful with poor Jake."

He kissed her again, another soft breath of a kiss. "Do you think you could learn to trust me, after all?"

She smiled against his mouth. "I don't have to learn that. I do trust you. Now."

His strong arms encircled her. "Shall I show you my estimates?"

She snuggled against him. "We'll get around to that."

"I'll try not to push too fast."

She sighed. "And some things I just don't want to change."

"That's fair. We'll work on compromise."

"Right along with sharing."

"Sounds good to me."

Cradled close against his heart, she looked up at him. "I love you. And I know now that you love me."

"Reading my mind again?"

"Am I wrong?"

"No, Ms. Sophie B. Jones. You are very, very right."

Epilogue

The next night, Oggie Jones appeared at the Mountain Star Theater.

One look at Sophie's face and he knew. "I guess I don't have to ask how things worked out with you and your man."

Before he left, he invited both of them to his eighty-first birthday party.

"We'll come," Sophie promised. "If you'll come to our wedding and give me away."

"You got yourselves a deal," the old man declared.

Three weeks later, on October ninth, Sin and Sophie attended Oggie's party at the Hole in the Wall Saloon. More than one toast was raised to the bride-and groom-to-be.

Sophie married Sin the following Saturday, the eleventh of October, in the Mountain Star Theater. A number of Joneses were there, including little Anthea, who somehow managed to wander off during the ceremony. A frantic search ensued. Jake, Caleb's new assistant, found the child at last—in the stable, unharmed, sitting on the stool beside Black Angel's stall.

Once everyone had stopped fussing over Anthea, Oggie admired the horse. Sin explained how he'd bought her for a song from a woman who'd decided owning a spirited horse wasn't for her.

The party in the cottage went on all night.

Oggie was the last guest to leave. When Sin and Sophie walked him out to his Cadillac, the sun had just raised its blinding face above the rim of the mountains to the east.

"Drive carefully," Sophie admonished him.

"I will. All the way to LA."

Sophie and Sin exchanged a look. "What's in LA?" they asked in unison.

"A nephew," the old man replied. "A nephew I haven't even met yet."

Sophie frowned. "Is he expecting you?"

Oggie pulled a cigar from his pocket. "Hell, gal." He peeled off the wrapper and bit off the end. "You oughta know by now that nobody's ever expectin' old Oggie Jones."

*   *   *   *   *

*Who is this nephew that Oggie
is going to surprise? He's Billy Jones,
and when it comes to surprises,
Oggie's is the least of it!
Read on for a sneak preview of*

THE TAMING OF BILLY JONES,

*Christine Rimmer's single title,
coming in October from Silhouette...*

The Taming of Billy Jones

The door stood open. Randi Wilding's sister—what the hell was her name: Verity? Constance?—was waiting for Billy behind her fancy inlaid mahogany desk, a stack of papers in front of her and one of those notebook computers at her elbow.

Beside Billy, the butler coughed discreetly. "Mr. Jones is here."

The woman looked up, those ugly glasses of hers magnifying her eyes in a way that made them seem to bulge. Her brownish hair was skinned back, her face scrubbed so clean it gave off a shine like a newly waxed floor. She reminded him of some giant, solemn insect—an insect that had somehow got itself all dressed up in a tidy gray business suit.

She flicked a bug-eye glance at the butler. "Thank you, Lance."

Lance gave a brief nod, then turned and strode off, leaving Randi's sister and Billy to stare at each other for a minuscule period of time that somehow, to Billy, seemed as if it went on for about two hundred years.

Finally, she spoke up. "I've been meaning to contact you. To be honest, as of yet, I hadn't quite gathered the courage."

Her words could mean only one thing: she knew Randi's kid was his.

Randi's kid was his. The reality hit him all over again, making his stomach churn and his knees turn to rubber.

He wondered bleakly what had come over him, to show up here, at the mansion Randi used to call home. Yes, he'd been putting up with a nightmare or two lately. And he was a little curious about the kid who looked so much like him.

But what the hell did he plan to do about it, now that the sister had as good as admitted the truth? He knew nothing about fatherhood—he *wanted* to know nothing about fatherhood.

The sister was looking at him through those scary magnified eyes of hers. "Please," she said. "Don't just stand there in the doorway staring at me as if I've committed some unconscionable crime. I'm sure, somehow, that we can work this out." She gestured toward a chair opposite her desk. "Sit down."

It was so damn quiet. He hated quiet. He wanted to ask the insect woman to turn on a little music, but there was no stereo in sight.

She gestured at the chair again. "Please."

He stepped over the threshold. "I'll stand."

She gave a tiny have-it-your-way shrug, then took off her glasses and rubbed the bridge of her nose. He watched her, feeling a fraction easier for the brief moment that she didn't have those eyes pinned on him.

But the moment ended all too soon. She settled the glasses back in place and folded her hands on her desk pad, which was one-hundred-percent free of doodles and smudges. "Mr. Jones. I...." Her voice broke. She looked away, then seemed to force herself to look at him again, and to go on. "I loved my sister. She was generous and funny. And talented. And...good." He saw defiance in her giant eyeballs, as if she dared him to say a bad word about Randi.

Billy had made a lot of mistakes in his life, but he wasn't about to make one right then. He kept his mouth shut, though he couldn't help picturing that famous shot from a certain men's magazine, that shot of Randi spread out on a zebra skin rug, wearing nothing but a diamond watch, a butterfly tattoo and a look of pure, unbridled lust.

Unaware of Billy's disrespectful thoughts, the sister continued, "Still, the fact is, she should have told you about the baby. I tried to convince her to tell you. But she felt you weren't cut out to be a father. That you had no *desire* to be a father. So when she found out she was pregnant, she—"

"Dumped me." He felt self-righteous, suddenly. It wasn't a bad feeling, especially not compared to scared spitless, which had been his basic emotional state since he entered that damn silent room. He let his lip curl a little, giving the woman a good, solid sneer. "She dumped me flat."

The sister flinched. "Let's just say she ended your...liaison."

Billy decided to enjoy being the wounded one. He had a right, the way he figured it. He *had* been kept in the dark. "That's a fancy way of putting it." He made a low sound in his throat, one intended to indicate his total disgust with the way he'd been treated. "But dumped is dumped, no matter how you try to gussy it up."

The woman's mouth pursed into a tight little bud. "Please. Randi did what she thought was right. And now she's gone. Now *I'm* Jesse's guardian. And I will do what *I* think is right."

Billy decided he felt a little too queasy to keep on standing, after all. He dropped into the chair opposite her, the one he'd refused a moment ago. He forced out his next words. "And what exactly do you think is right?"

"Well...." She patted the tight little bun at the back of her neck and fiddled with her glasses some more.

"Well, what?" he demanded, pleased at how dangerous he sounded, since he felt about as menacing as limp spaghetti.

She gulped and blinked. "Mr. Jones, I think your son should know you."

"What the hell does that mean?"

"It means I think he should have a chance to build some kind of relationship with you. I think..." The sentence kind of ran out of steam. She leaned toward him, frowning.

He threatened her by deepening his scowl. "What?"

She seemed to have forgotten that he was scaring her. A strange, soft look came over her. The corners of her mouth turned up slowly in a tender smile. For a moment, even with those bug eyes, she was pretty.

Then she said, "You're terrified."

He realized that he hated her.

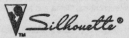

Take 2 bestselling love stories FREE
Plus get a FREE surprise gift!

Special Limited-Time Offer

Mail to Silhouette Reader Service™

P.O. Box 609
Fort Erie, Ontario
L2A 5X3

YES! Please send me 2 free Silhouette Special Edition® novels and my free surprise gift. Then send me 6 brand-new novels every month, which I will receive months before they appear in bookstores. Bill me at the low price of $3.96 each plus 25¢ delivery and GST*. That's the complete price, and a saving of over 10% off the cover prices—quite a bargain! I understand that accepting the books and gift places me under no obligation ever to buy any books. I can always return a shipment and cancel at any time. Even if I never buy another book from Silhouette, the 2 free books and the surprise gift are mine to keep forever.

335 SEN CH7X

_____

Name   (PLEASE PRINT)

_____

Address   Apt. No.

_____

City   Province   Postal Code

This offer is limited to one order per household and not valid to present Silhouette Special Edition® subscribers. *Terms and prices are subject to change without notice.
Canadian residents will be charged applicable provincial taxes and GST.

CSPED-98   ©1990 Harlequin Enterprises Limited

Bestselling author
Joan Elliott Pickart launches
Silhouette's newest cross-line promotion

Follow That Baby!

with
THE
RANCHER
AND
THE
AMNESIAC
BRIDE
Special Edition,
October 1998

Josie Wentworth of the oil-rich Oklahoma Wentworths knew penthouse apartments and linen finery—not working ranches...and certainly *not* remote, recalcitrant ranchers! But one conk to the head and one slight case of amnesia had this socialite beauty sharing time and tangling sheets with the cowboy least likely to pop the question....

And don't miss **The Daddy and the Baby Doctor** by Kristin Morgan, when FOLLOW THAT BABY! continues in Silhouette Romance in November 1998!

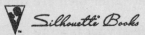

Silhouette Books

Available at your favorite retail outlet.

**Available October 1998
from Silhouette Books...**

World's Most
Eligible Bachelors

DETECTIVE DAD
by Marie Ferrarella

The World's Most Eligible Bachelor: Undercover
agent Duncan MacNeill, a wealthy heir with a taut
body...and an even harder heart.

Duncan MacNeill just got the toughest assignment
of his life: deliver a beautiful stranger's baby in the
back seat of her car! This tight-lipped loner never
intended to share his name with anyone—
especially a mystery woman who claimed to have a
total memory loss. But how long could he hope to
resist succumbing to the lure of daddyhood—
and marriage?

**Each month, Silhouette Books brings you
a brand-new story about an absolutely
irresistible bachelor. Find out how the sexiest,
most sought-after men are finally caught.**

Available at your favorite retail outlet.

Silhouette®

Look us up on-line at: http://www.romance.net   PSWMEB2

MATERNITY LEAVE

Coming September 1998

Three delightful stories about the blessings
and surprises of "Labor" Day.

TABLOID BABY by Candace Camp

She was whisked to the hospital in the nick of time....

THE NINE-MONTH KNIGHT
by Cait London

A down-on-her-luck secretary is experiencing
odd little midnight cravings....

THE PATERNITY TEST by Sherryl Woods

The stick turned blue before her
biological clock struck twelve....

*These three special women are very pregnant...and very
single, although they won't be either for too much longer,
because baby—and Daddy—are on their way!*

Available at your favorite retail outlet.

Silhouette Romance
celebrates the joys
of first love in

VIRGIN BRIDES

September 1998:
THE GUARDIAN'S BRIDE
by Laurie Paige (#1318)
A young heiress, desperately in love with her
older, wealthy guardian, dreams of wedding the
tender tycoon. But he has plans to marry
her off to another....

October 1998:
THE NINE-MONTH BRIDE
by Judy Christenberry (#1324)
A widowed rancher who wants an heir and a prim librarian
who wants a baby decide to marry for convenience—but will
motherhood make this man and wife rethink their
temporary vows?

November 1998:
A BRIDE TO HONOR by Arlene James (#1330)
A pretty party planner falls for a charming, honor-bound
millionaire who's being roped into a loveless marriage. When
the wedding day arrives, will *she* be his blushing bride?

December 1998:
A KISS, A KID AND A MISTLETOE BRIDE (#1336)
When a scandalous single dad returns home at
Christmas, he encounters the golden girl he'd fallen
for one magical night a lifetime before.

Available at your favorite retail outlet.

We, the undersigned, having barely survived four years of nursing school, do hereby vow to meet at Granetti's at least once a week, not to do anything drastic to our hair without consulting each other first and never, _ever_—no matter how rich, how cute, how funny, how smart, or how good in bed—marry a doctor.

Dana Rowan, R.N.
Lee Murphy, R.N.
Katie Sheppard, R.N.

Christine Flynn
Susan Mallery
Christine Rimmer

prescribe a massive dose of heart-stopping romance in their scintillating new series, **PRESCRIPTION: MARRIAGE**. Three nurses are determined _not_ to wed doctors— only to discover the men of their dreams come with a medical degree!

Look for this unforgettable series in fall 1998:

October 1998: **FROM HOUSE CALLS TO HUSBAND** by Christine Flynn

November 1998: **PRINCE CHARMING, M.D.** by Susan Mallery

December 1998: **DR. DEVASTATING** by Christine Rimmer

Only from

Silhouette®SPECIAL EDITION®

Available at your favorite retail outlet.